The *Anxiety*
of Everyday Objects

The *Anxiety*

of Everyday Objects

·

A NOVEL

Aurelie Sheehan

Penguin Books

PENGUIN BOOKS
Published by the Penguin Group
Penguin Group (USA) Inc., 375 Hudson Street,
New York New York 10014, U.S.A.
Penguin Books Ltd, 80 Strand,
London WC2R 0RL, England
Penguin Books Australia Ltd, 250 Camberwell Road, Camberwell,
Victoria 3124, Australia
Penguin Books Canada Ltd, 10 Alcorn Avenue,
Toronto, Ontario, Canada M4V 3B2
Penguin Books India (P) Ltd, 11 Community Centre, Panchsheel Park,
New Delhi - 110 017, India
Penguin Books (N.Z.) Ltd, Cnr Rosedale and Airborne Roads, Albany,
Auckland, New Zealand
Penguin Books (South Africa) (Pty) Ltd, 24 Sturdee Avenue,
Rosebank, Johannesburg 2196, South Africa

Penguin Books Ltd, Registered Offices:
80 Strand, London WC2R 0RL, England

First published in Penguin Books 2004

1 3 5 7 9 10 8 6 4 2

LIBRARY OF CONGRESS CATALOGING IN PUBLICATION DATA
Sheehan, Aurelie, 1963–
The anxiety of everyday objects : a novel / Aurelie Sheehan.
p.   cm.
ISBN 0 14 20.0370 0
I. Title.
PS3569.H392155A83 2004
813'.54—dc21   2003049873

Printed in the United States of America
Set in Janson MT with Adobe Jenson Italic
Designed by Sabrina Bowers

For Reed

Acknowledgments

Gratitude and love to all my family, and in particular to my husband, Reed, who has helped me with this book more than I can say. I also benefited from the comments and encouragement of my friends. Early readers included Peter Rock, Susan Thames, and Jason Brown, as well as Gail Somers Sun, Janice K. Johnson, Cecily and Car olanne Patterson. Thanks also to Howard Norman for his insight at a crucial stage. It's an honor to work with Ellen Levine and Molly Stern, fierce and elegant defenders of the word. Love to Alexandra, who brings me joy.

Contents ～

Sincerity

In which the heroine establishes herself

1

All good secretaries will eventually find truth in the hearts of men.

Winona Bartlett, Win to her friends, might not have been the world's best secretary, but her nature was such that serving, subservience, and coffee service came easily, and, in fact, she felt there was an inherent good in doing things well, and this determination more than equaled her actual interest in the long-term prospects at Grecko Mauster Crill. She practiced her secretarial role as a Zen meditation; what role she was more suited to remained a mystery, though she was now nearly thirty. She held on to the notion that one day she might make a living by creative, individualistic endeavor. It was her belief that if she in fact made the pretty God's eye with purple and orange yarn and winsomely presented her creation, the judge would be charmed, and she would get a gold star.

Or so it seemed to have been promised to our heroine, who at this moment was standing on an elevator, soaring up to the Chrysler Building's fifty-eighth floor.

That's not to say she wasn't smart in the world—Winona had done fine in school and by the time she landed at the law firm, she had revised her résumé at least twenty times, honing it and adding to it carefully, as if it were a house of cards. But some of her greatest moments of glory weren't in there. For instance, in college, when the DJ invited her to co-emcee the dance with him and she wore a swirling '50s dress and red lipstick and said sassy and amplified things to throngs of bisexual castabouts. You could say she considered it a triumph when she cast surly, unpleasant Ronald in her "Avant-Garde Film History and Techniques" final project, a Super-8 film about a woman who is "afraid to be revealed" and ultimately disappears when she throws her diary into a river. Or perhaps you might consider her interview techniques a plus. When she bluffed her way into the film program, for example, or when she put on a long floral dress and matching green pumps from Shoe Town and told the lawyers, *I am a good secretary*, and then asked for twice as much money as she'd ever made as a waitress or as the assistant to the assistant at the bookstore.

If you are wondering if she is pretty, this is the story. When she was in eighth grade she'd speculated on this subject, twice in particular: once, upon being surrounded and interrogated by a group of girls in her new school, she said yes, she thought she was pretty. Later that same year, in a more casual moment with a friend and a camp counselor, she revealed that actually she thought she was, well, *pretty* pretty. She didn't stand out as a bombshell—maybe a Miss Moneypenny. Her hair was cut in a bob, and she sometimes flipped a section over to the other side in a happy and unruly flop. She wore a little makeup, eye pencil and a touch of lipstick, and today, her Queen Elizabeth perfume (some scents said *stay away,* some said *come closer*). Even in her well-matched outfit and pantyhose, she looked slightly out of place in the business world. She was no East Village leather mama; no strange-fruit lipstick or ball-and-chain fashion statements on Winona. But she was willowy, and she moved like a gazelle, and there was about her, you couldn't miss it, a betraying twinge of bohemia.

It was reassuring to be on the elevator with the goers and getters of the universe, to catch a glimpse of her reflection in the gleaming enclosure, a worker bee like all the others. Still, Winona stood rather rigidly in her new, like-everyone-else trench coat—waist, toes, underarms itchy with Monday-morning alarm.

•

Law office décor: dark, manly. A brown leather couch took up one side of the reception area, and on the other you had a pair of armchairs and a sleek coffee table, *The New Republic, Time,* and *Fortune* arrayed there like a spread hand of winning cards. Lucy's desk was empty—she was almost never on time—and an ominously large oil painting of one of the firm's founding partners loomed over her unattended phone and paper clip holder: Anthony Grecko, Esquire, sitting cross-legged in a high-backed chair, his hands folded, his head teetering forward. A lone windbreaker hung from the coat stand in the corner, as it had for months. (As per Nancy's request, employees hung their coats in the storage room, by the photocopier.)

"Good morning, Nancy," Winona said, peering into the first office down the hall. A fecund haze surrounded the door.

Nancy Hobbs, office manager, raised orchids on her windowsill, and the flowers exuded a tropical torpor, some sort of barely contained hothouse hysteria. Winona liked but was disconcerted by the heat and odor, the orchids tangled and sexy in a southern belle/Catholic guilt sort of way. And then there was something about the way Nancy was about the orchids, or, to be honest, just about Nancy.

"Good morning," the older woman said, leaning forward, clasping her hands together.

A lapis necklace hung around Nancy's neck, beads strung like captives from an exotic land. Her short hair curled in troubled wisps under her ears. Nancy was half-administrative and half-professional. This made her crazy; it was the curse of the ill defined. It was impossible not to be saddened by the sight of Nancy scurrying about, pinning lavender to bulletin boards.

"How was your weekend?" Winona asked.

The question seemed to surprise, or at least vaguely offend. Perhaps Nancy didn't want to think of her weekend anymore. Some people like Monday morning most of all. She turned her head toward the windowsill, to her delicate, moss-scented flowers. Her hands were too firmly clasped together.

"Too short," she finally said.

"So true," Winona said.

"It's going to be a busy day," Nancy commented. "I've been here since seven, working away like a little mouse in her corner, a little spinning mouse who never has a moment to spare."

"Ahh," said Winona.

Rex wasn't at his desk, but his jacket was half falling from the back of his chair. Umar's office was empty. (Of Umar, anyway—a footpath to the chair was the only clear space in the room; everything else was stacked with correspondence, pleadings, rulings, depositions, affidavits, requests, motions, briefs, interrogatories, agreements, disagreements, contracts, and magazines, mostly—to Winona's consternation—*Penthouse.*) At the end of the hall, in the corner office, William Mauster hunched over his desk like a creature from *Where the Wild Things Are.*

•

Winona's Workshop, they might have called her room, or Winona's Catch-All Area. This was where Grecko Mauster Crill stored the file cabinets, printer, secretary, and scanner. Doorless, its architecture emphasized accessibility: the back of the room was open to the hall, and above Winona's desk a large window had been cut out of the white plaster. Winona called this her Mr. Ed window, the place where lawyers could lean in, survey, and query. From it, she could see through the conference room and out the window to another skyscraper.

She dropped her purse in the warren between printer and workstation, then sat down on her swiveling chair. Her computer played a familiar song as it booted up, a reveille for the office worker. The phone rang; it was Winona's sister.

"Hello, Liz," Winona said with a slightly false breeziness. She had last spoken to Liz the night before.

She could almost tell Liz's mood from the pause before she spoke, let alone from the tone of her voice. She could tell her sister's mood with her eyes closed, ears plugged with Play-Doh, and French fries up her nostrils.

"What are you doing?" Liz asked.

"Well, I just got to work."

"I know this is totally crazy, but I've got my tennis lesson tonight, and I can't decide whether to wear my hair up, in a ponytail out the back of my cap, or down, with no cap."

"I'm sure either way would look very nice, Liz."

"If I wear the ponytail, maybe Kevin would think I was trying to look younger. But I am proud of my age—and fuck him!"

"Um—good point!"

"Are you listening? It sounds like you're doing something else."

Winona took her hands off the keyboard.

"I'm listening."

"Maybe I should call back when you can pay attention. Will you be home later? Around six?"

Winona was afraid she probably would be home. Home was a studio apartment with one large clock her mother had given her. It was a white clock with imposing black numerals. It hung in the kitchen area (the wall clustered with a little refrigerator, sink, and stove—a Dolly Madison Play Kitchen). The clock ticked too loudly for comfort and, worse, it ticked faster on the downswing. *Tick. Tick. Tick. TICKTICKTICK.* It was slowly driving Winona insane. She sometimes wondered if she should take it down, not for her own sake, but for Fruit Bat's. Fruit Bat was a cat, a good cat—she had told him so just that morning, whispering in his black, bat-wing ear.

"Sure, I'll be there."

"Okay, well, I'll talk to you then."

"Okay, bye."

She hung up and stared, briefly, into empty space, a distinctly non-breezy feeling in the air. She snapped out of it and checked her e-mail—nothing to speak of. One from the bookkeeper, one from her mother.

•

Bill was standing, leaning toward the phone in a way that made it seem he was about to get off. He was obviously talking to Doug Sandwitz, the Stratosphere lawyer.

"Yeah, we all love settlement. Settlement is beautiful. Communication is beautiful. But *you* fucked *us* over, remember? Stratosphere has no right to *any* of that market. Not *any* of it. Generosity? Goodwill? Market share? Ha! Ha! Ha! Lisa Box didn't just *start* the beauty kiosk, Lisa Box *is* the beauty kiosk."

Grecko Mauster Crill was a small, general practice, and most of its clients were run of the mill: you had your basic pizza franchise, your doctor with his investments, your real estate transfers, corporate setups, a handful of pro bono criminals (sometimes they'd come in wearing jeans and smelling like vodka—didn't these boys know how to pretend?). Then you had Lisa Box, Inc.—the big,

9

the glorious, the innovative, and now, the nearly bank-rupt. Every time Bill talked to Sandwitz, the lawyer for Lisa Box's main rival, it sounded like this. Ravenous.

Then again, Bill's sweetie-pie skills were a bit lacking in general.

He fumed while Sandwitz, apparently, made some retort. Then: "Mall schmall . . . you know and I know what your client is trying to do—what you're trying to do, my friend."

Click.

"Good morning, Mr. Mauster."

Winona stood poised at his door, nearly tiptoeing, nearly falling over. It was an eager stance, the stance of the over-pleaser. She was presenting herself: a young woman doing unflaggingly well in her role, taking her job extremely seriously, not even feeling overeducated or mis-placed or any of those troublesome responses likely to plague the artsy English-major types who find their way into the secretarial paddock. Everyone has to make a living, even fledgling filmmakers. Is there one kind of job that's better than another? At least she was no longer dueting with a yellow plastic bucket on wheels and a hairy mop like she did at the restaurant. She stood like the thirty-ninth runner-up in a beauty contest, professional in her black skirt and black-and-white gauzy blouse, even fashion-able—her square-toed pumps topped with whimsically large buckles, her nail polish a cunning shade of silver.

"Morning," said the lawyer, searching his desk for something.

Remember *Bleak House,* three thousand pages long and featuring thirty or forty lawyers? Winona read it in school, though she didn't recall much of it, except for the peculiar admiration it evoked in her pink-cheeked professor. Still, there was a resemblance to one shadowy lawyer from that novel in Mr. Mauster. He was shaped like a hill in a bog. He was shaped like Sasquatch, humped and hunkered over in a mythical brooding funk.

"Would you like some coffee? I've got a fresh pot on."

"That would be . . ."

Bill Mauster started reading a letter and trailed off.

When she first came to the firm, Winona had been instructed by Bill Mauster on the exact strength at which he preferred his coffee. If she didn't mind, could she please make a pot every morning? He told her about the nine teaspoons, all heaped just so, not *towers*, per se, but *mounds* of Colombian. She encountered mystifying, unnerving inconsistency with the method. Mr. Mauster would sometimes complain, sometimes praise, but she always did it the same way. She'd take the first sip in the morning and a small, undeniable clutch of anxiety would take hold of her if it seemed too weak or too strong. This morning, as all mornings, he would say yes, bring him the coffee. Still, it was Winona and Bill's ritual to make a question out of this answer. As a successful secretary, she initiated the communiqué.

Winona scanned the sprawl of windows behind Bill. Manhattan, a Mondrian checkerboard of grays, a jigsaw of blue. Her gaze returned to the brooding lawyer.

"Sir?" she prompted.

"Yes?"

"Coffee?"

"Yes, wonderful, terrific."

Bill's favorite mug was missing from the storage-room shelf, and this gave Winona pause. Should she go back and bother him, looking around his office to find the mug, possibly left from Friday, a pox of mold floating on an inch of dead, cold coffee? Or should she give him his second-favorite mug, the burgundy-and-white one with the Harvard insignia? Boldly, Winona made her decision—she took the Harvard mug off the shelf. She retrieved the milk, deftly pouring in the required amount: enough to besmirch, not to cool down. Then a teaspoon—a *level* teaspoon—of sugar. She glided back down the hall.

The weekend had been filled with the chaos of loneliness: transplanting a geranium, not going to the block party, avoiding close encounters with Jeremy the Sincere. Winona walked down the hall and felt a surge of emotion: *I belong here.* All would be right in the world if Mr. Mauster liked his coffee this morning, if she had gotten the proportions right on the milk and sugar.

2

She had ducked him on Friday, but then when the sun started to go down on Saturday afternoon, she panicked slightly, the sky darkening around her, an unchecked chill in the air. Winona returned the calls of Jeremy the Sincere. You could say they were going out together; you could even say they were going steady (a little *too* steady), but freedom still rung through her weekend. She could pretend to be doing something she was not; she could speak about it in somewhat vague terms, and hope that later no further explanation would be required.

That night, they went out to dinner.

"Maybe I should move to L.A."

"L.A.?" Jeremy asked, as if she had just said GN or SW or LQ, but then he checked himself and said, "I'd support any decision that was right for you."

Winona smiled. There was something beautiful about a person who would say such a thing. And even if there wasn't, there was the fact that he did have lovely shoulders. And even if he didn't have lovely shoulders, there was the fact that they got along so well, and they liked many of the same movies. And he certainly knew a lot about theater, and had an appreciation of, if not a flair for, fashion. He had lived in New York for ten years, and she'd only been there three. Surely there was a kind of accumulation of NYC, all that it stood for—the *je ne sais quoi* of the ubiquitous blue-and-gold Turkish-Greek coffee cup and the buttered rolls—in a man such as this. A man working toward his Ph.D.; writing for off-off-off Broadway; temping for an art administrator (a fellow traveler!). And even if he *hadn't* been from New York, there was the fact that he was a human. And the fact that humans are, inherently, lovable.

And he was kind to her.

Even if he didn't want to have sex . . . yet.

He was still getting over . . . something.

It had nothing to do with his bisexuality, he'd told her.

"Thank you, Jeremy, thank you," Winona said. "Although, when I really think about it, I don't know. Too many screenwriters live in L.A. I don't want to be a screenwriter, per se, but I want to use film as a canvas. Be an artist, sort of."

"I'm listening."

"But I'm sure every screenwriter thinks that way."

Jeremy stroked his goatee. It was a time when goatees had just come back into fashion, when their wearers went beyond the Transylvanian and the physicist. In her life,

Winona had kissed two men with hair around their lips. It was okay. It was like kissing a hamster.

"Do you agree?" she asked.

"I think so. I can only speak for myself, a denizen of the theater."

"Oh, come on, go out on a limb."

"Screen, stage, canvas, page—they are all so different, Winona. How can we ever make comparisons?"

"It seems you could, if you used your imagination."

Jeremy hunched slightly, there at their table for two. Entrées could be purchased for $5.99 here. The small bouquet of fabric flowers on the butcher-block tabletop was furred with residual garlic and clove.

Jeremy looked back up with his sleepy eyes. "But I *am* using my imagination."

"Oh, I know you are," said Winona. "I just meant—" She knocked his elbow. "You know!"

Winona had read in an article that it was good, healthy, not to fall in love too soon. She and Jeremy had been dating, in their way, for three months. It seemed that he wanted to date the old fashioned way, with lots of Getting to Know Each Other. Winona liked the water but feared the approach—she'd just as soon dive in, not this toe-to-knee-to-thigh technique. Acclimation did not thrill, it startled: the excruciating discomfort, the unbearable self-consciousness of it all!

"I know. I'm sorry. I'm just feeling a little, I don't know, vulnerable tonight."

"Why?" Winona asked. "Why are you feeling vulnerable?"

Their meals arrived, eggplant and chickpeas and bulgur. (Would they feel less vulnerable if, tonight, they ate a little steak?)

Jeremy picked up his fork. He prodded the eggplant thoughtfully, to see if it was alive. He shrugged. "I had a meeting with my committee yesterday, and it didn't go that well."

"What happened?"

"Well, Helmut doesn't like the premise of my third chapter. He doesn't think Williams is . . ."

He went on for a while. Winona was glad people were still studying literature, reading plays, talking about the intellect and the psyche and the line break. She understood, as well, that Jeremy's concerns were founded. Tonight he was wearing his favorite shirt, red with purple stars on it. He had bought it at Urban Outfitters; he wore it with a certain pride; it was his dress shirt.

They were small stars.

•

Do I believe that most people are inherently good, that they will, if given the chance, be nice? Or could it be true that each one of us is representative of the entire organism, and so that if good and evil exist in the whole, there is at least some of each in every one of us? Do I believe in categories? What do they have to do with a satisfying life? What about men and women? Are they at odds? What about sex? There is no union without division, correct? Life couldn't go on? Why do I feel like my head's going to blow off?

Winona mulled these things over in a furious little gerbil-on-the-treadmill panic. Were they, perhaps, or could they be made, cinematic? Jeremy was sitting in bed next to her, reading *Three Critics Speak: The Shadow in Theatre.*

"I don't know," she said.

"What, dear?"

He just called her dear. But not the way a father or a sexy criminal would say it. No, more like the way Mr. Rabbit would say it to Mrs. Rabbit. Winona turned on her side. She put her hand on his leg.

"I'm feeling a little, you know," she said.

Jeremy looked straight above his book for a moment, and then placed it down on his knees. Then he moved it over to her nightstand. He turned on his side, facing her, and bent his knees slightly and leaned on his elbow.

"You are, huh?" He hesitated again, and then kissed her on the nose.

•

Lisa Box, Inc., was, in a sense, a good idea. At least, Winona had nodded enthusiastically as Bill and Umar had described it to her during her early days at the firm, and when she met Ron Blitzen and Leo Grogon for the first time she admired the fact that these two, perhaps inauspicious, men—the former accountant at a "gentleman's club" and a hairdresser—could have tapped into a market that was obviously ready to be discovered. She herself had always thought more could be made of those numbing airport hours. They provided an excellent opportunity for a manicure, for instance, but she'd only seen a nail salon once, on her way to Vancouver.

The first Lisa Box was in Miami International Airport. Physically, it resembled a pod from outer space. Within it lurked a woman willing to criticize.

This was how it worked: the client was first given a quick interview by a Life Specialist. The questions were important, but really the critical one was analyzing the other woman's speech, mannerisms, and overall demeanor. Then the client stood in a coffin-like enclosure hooked up with all sorts of prods and receptors that tested for fat density, skin tone, skin color, hair color, hair consistency—everything that can be measured. This information, along with certain important and secret prompts known only to the Life Specialist, was entered into the computer and sent to a panel of beauty specialists (a physical trainer, a makeup artist, a fashion designer, and a recent college graduate, usually a handsome athlete-type) via teleconference—this was the Upgrade Panel. The panel asked the client a couple of clarifying questions, pinpointing her insecurities and expectations, and then made a series of pronouncements. Then the TV was clicked off and the Life Specialist gave a Judge Judy-type summary of the client in these categories:

Ready!: the client's makeup, clothes, and facial/body shape
Set!: the client's self-presentation, articulation, and charisma quotient
Go!: the client's best-bet options in love and work, based on the above

Suggestions for products, services, and altered personal habits were printed out, along with computer-simulated pictures of Upgraded You, and then stuffed in a folder along with product and service coupons. Cosmetic surgery options—breast augmentation, tummy tucks, collagen injections—all came with handy discounts.

The client's life had been transformed. She was out a hundred bucks and thirty minutes, but she could still make it to Des Moines by four.

It was like having the most beautiful girl in high school come up and tell you, for real, why no one asked you to the prom. It was like your ex-boyfriends telling you why, other than "they need space," you were not quite up to par.

Everything at Lisa Box, Inc. was rosy for a while. Leo and Ron opened thirty locations and were making money hand over fist—every dollar they made from a woman in need was matched or surpassed by cash coming in from product and service endorsements. This left them flush, even after they gave money to their associated charity, Lisa's Lil' Sister.

Then Leo split off from Lisa Box.

When Ron found out about Leo's new beauty kiosk company, Stratosphere, he went completely ballistic. Winona remembered Bill trying to calm him down, then Umar going in, then Umar closing the door. When they emerged, it was with the smiling faces of those who were about to sue the ass off of someone near and dear.

The problem was that the trial was still two months away, and Lisa Box was losing business. Ron hadn't paid his legal fees in three months. Bill and Umar hadn't paid themselves in that long, though they'd kept the staff paychecks coming. Ron now owed the firm more than two hundred thousand dollars, mostly Lisa Box related, but also because his wife—the lovely Brenda Blitzen, one of the first Lisa Box success stories—had recently sued him for divorce after a series of, well, inscrutable moments between herself and Ron, most of which seemed to involve one or the other of them flying off to tropical islands or switching cell phone numbers or staying for indeterminate periods of time at hotels.

•

Work swept over Winona like the feeling of being anesthetized for minor ear surgery as a child, gas mask over her mouth, the not-pleasant but not-bad feeling of a whole different world, a No World. Grecko Mauster Crill filled her head with its insistent, numbing importance. Jeremy couldn't fill such a void, though he tried in his own small way. On the other hand, she wasn't too keen on the other guy she had recently accompanied on a date, to prove to herself she was still in the mix. At a friend's party, he came up and said, "Let's go out this Saturday. I'll show you the real Manhattan." "Okay," she'd answered, too baffled to resist. At lunch he got ketchup on his sleeve and she watched the red spot as he brought the hamburger to and from his mouth and told her, in a patronizing tone, what each neighborhood in Manhattan *meant*, how it got that way, and why he would buy an apartment on the Upper West Side before the East Side now, though in the *seventies* it was a different story. On the sidewalk, after the movie (which he'd paid for with an unnatural flourish), he'd held Winona's arm tight as she was backing up. "Don't I deserve a good-bye kiss?" he asked. And the question hung in the air.

Now Winona typed her thousandth letter to Doug Sandwitz regarding *Lisa Box v. Stratosphere*.

"Did I ever mention that you look like Audrey Hepburn?"

It was Rex, leaning in the Mr. Ed window.

"That's just crazy talk, Rex. But tell me, how was your weekend, young sport?"

Rex Willard's dark blond hair waved back from his face as if he were in a wind machine. Most mornings his face was ghostly pale. Color came after lunch. He was the young up-and-coming lawyer, the only associate under Bill and Umar. They ran him around like mad, and he was dedicated and smart and hardworking, if not a little cynical and harried. The careful observer could see that small infractions in the status quo made him glad. He was always bugging Winona. He seemed to think she had gotten further in "Arts and Leisure" than he had. He also liked her "Week in Review." He asked her questions about sentence construction, how to use the postage meter, what to wear to the theater. Mostly he just stole her newspaper.

"Oh—my weekend. Grim! Very grim. You don't want to know."

"Really? Grim ill? Grim boring? Grim romantic?"

"Of all the gin joints in New York, she had to come into mine."

"Ahh—grim romantic."

"A person might think so, but no, just grim grim. You could say tequila had something to do with it."

"Tequila, in February?" she asked.

"Yeah, so?"

"I think of it as a summer drink."

"Maybe—if you're not drinking it straight from the bottle. So, how was your weekend?"

"Exciting—the geranium really seems to match the new pot."

Winona liked Rex—as a brother. The phrase would

have made him groan. There was nothing worse than being liked in that fraternal way, after all. Winona thought of him as one-third mathematician, one-third philosopher, and one-third derelict—always half-resisting the job he excelled in. He was a year her junior, and they lived in different Manhattans. Uptown, he had brunch, debutantes, L'Occitane soap boutiques, dogs with their own psychotherapists. She could claim bialys, Chihuahuas, cheap socks, and video stores carrying *Zazie in the Metro* and *Kiss the Girls Goodbye*. But they met in the middle, here on Lexington Avenue. Winona's outer calm, an instinct to whistle when she walked, at times entirely hid her anxiety, her internal sense of disaster. With Rex, the calm thing was more real, came easier. This, even though he was a lawyer. One of *them*. A suit-wearer.

"Excellent sign! Come on, you probably went to half a dozen of those downtown roof parties or whatever. Or maybe some movie director took you to dinner."

"Well, let's see. I read a little."

"Have you read Grisham's new one?"

"John Grisham? I don't read John Grisham."

"You don't?"

"No."

"Why not? He's cool. He's a *lawyer*."

"Are you insane? I read enough lawyers."

"No, really." Rex pounded his palms on the sill. "Read him," he said, leaning over in a fake threatening way.

"I'm more interested in your drunken revelry."

"I'm more interested in my BonPizza employment contract. C'mon, Hepburn, get back to work," he said, then leaned in and took her newspaper.

3 ⌢

The Grecko Mauster Crill conference room had a table bigger than many New York City apartments, made of a lustrous cherry wood so highly polished that flipped paper clips whizzed across its surface, and if you dropped a brief or an agreement it swished off into the hinterlands, never to return. When Nancy was there, you could not put a coffee mug directly on its surface, that's what the faux-British coasters (portraying herbs) were for. Nancy had suggested to Winona that, when Sandy Spires showed up, she give her a careful assessment. "The good secretary," Nancy had said, "always knows more about what's going on with people than her boss does. It's her job to impart this knowledge, all the while allowing the boss to think it's his observation or idea."

Her letter had come by fax last week, in the wake of

the first good news Bill Mauster and the firm had received in months.

Bill had gotten a call from a man named Blane Rasmussen. At his initial consultation with Bill and Umar, Blane described the corporate restructuring he envisioned for his company, Palm Consulting, and outlined as well a fair amount of ongoing legal issues he'd need to attend to in the next year. He was, it seemed, fabulously wealthy, an older man in a sky-blue shirt and tasseled loafers, and he was willing to pay above the norm for the firm's services on one condition: that they work in concert with Sandy Spires, a lone-wolf attorney Blane had become acquainted with recently. Ms. Spires had originally recommended Grecko Mauster Crill to Blane, and it would only be right to reward her with the work. Besides, she was extraordinarily good, he had said, with a passionate look in his eye.

Bill had lunch with her himself on Friday and had been impressed—so impressed that he was considering inviting her to work with the firm as consulting attorney, primarily working with Palm but also doing a few other things. Today's appointment was to discuss that further, with Bill as well as with Umar.

Winona had studied the fax on her way down the hall to Bill's office. *And should we have the pleasure of working together,* Sandy Spires had written, *you will be surprised at how inappropriate the moniker "disabled" can be.* Winona squinted at the signature—all boxy and small. She'd never seen a blind person's handwriting before. She'd never really met a blind person. How fascinating, how unusual, what an opportunity—but didn't you have to see to work here? It seemed like an all-body kind of thing. Could you slowly pare down sight, hearing, and ability to speak, and still get the job done? Was there an essential core to work in the law firm that had no relationship to the senses, that was just there, a central engine, like willpower, or greed?

Winona was straightening out the little island of office supplies in the middle of the table—phone, coasters, message pad, pens—when Lucy buzzed her on the intercom. Ms. Spires had arrived.

All right, then. She'd first speak and then shake hands, putting her hand out and, if nothing happened, tapping the woman's arm in a friendly sort of way. But would she want to be led? Would it be an insult to ask, or not to ask? Winona wasn't certain; maybe she should just say *Follow me*.

She turned the corner and saw, standing in the center of the reception area, a woman in silver: a breathtaking Sandy Spires. Winona hadn't expected her to be beautiful. From behind her wire-rimmed, delicately mod, silver-blue sunglasses, Sandy seemed to be looking right at her.

"Winona Bartlett," she said in a throaty murmur.

"Yes, hello, Ms. Spires?" Winona said, walking forward. Sandy Spires put out her hand. They shook; Sandy's hand was strong as a barber's.

"Nice to meet you. And I've already met Lucy." She turned her head toward the receptionist. "We've discovered we're both from Virginia."

"How nice!" Winona said.

Lucy arched her eyebrows.

Sandy Spires gazed—seemed to gaze—forward. Her shimmering suit poured over her like water. She wore silky herringbone knit stockings and slate-gray boots, a cross between *Little House on the Prairie* and *Star Trek*. Her close-fitting jacket was buttoned up, and at her throat tumbled out a whiff of white fabric. Her face was perfectly oval and her hair lay in wobbling blond ridges, stray curls escaping from both sides. Winona eyed the red tip of her long white stick, still moving back and forth like the impatient hoof of a race horse.

"I'll take you to the conference room, and I'm sure Mr. Mauster and Mr. Crill will be with you in just a minute. First, though, may I get you anything? Water, coffee?"

"Oh, I appreciate it, Winona. But no thanks."

"Okay. Well, then, shall I lead you down the hall?"

"I really don't need to be led." An intoxicating river of smooth words.

"All right, sure," said Winona, and turned. For some contrary-to-logical reason, she took long, slow steps, as if silence were recommended here. She stopped twice to see how Sandy was proceeding. She was coming along fine, and the glittery glare she gave Winona each time she paused, her silvery, egg-shaped glasses flashing, had a trace of coolness, even anger.

•

"We can sit here at the end of the table. Here's a chair for you, and I'll sit here."

Winona pulled out a chair, but the blind woman felt for, then ran her hand lightly down the back of, another chair, her own selection, and pulled it toward her. She sat down, clasped her hands in her lap, and set her profile against the picture-window view of New York. This was just like in the job training video! Winona felt optimistic, for they had, without incident, gotten down the hall.

"So you're the secretary, right? We talked once on the phone."

"Yup, I'm the secretary, just the secretary," said Winona, more or less cheerfully.

There was the possibility that she was a filmmaker, an artist. But that's not what she got paid for.

Sandy Spires seemed to be regarding her. Her nostrils, little snotless teacups, flared.

"Not *just* the secretary. You've got an important job. Overlooked, mostly. But the secretaries of the world keep things together. One thing's certain, you're always at the center of the news."

"That's kind of you to say," said Winona.

"I'm not kind, I'm honest. I, for one, rely on my staff like you wouldn't believe."

"Well, I'd be glad to help you in any way I can," Winona said, honored to think of helping this woman. She could photocopy. She could get the stapler. But she could also just, well, *serve*.

"Sandy," Bill said from the doorway, like he was calling out the name of a contestant who had won a car. "I'd like you to meet my partner, Umar."

Umar Crill (at his finest, meeting a new girl!) tossed his curly gray hair. He was, at times like these, both his real age and that of a high school rugby player, hopeful and handsome and unshowered. The man loved women. He loved women like closing your eyes and listening to the same—always the same—opera. He loved their raw, tender exposure to even the most ordinary things. It was divinity: the way a woman held a pen, when she was writing, on the back of her card, her home number.

Umar and Bill descended on Sandy like they were taking over a country. She remained seated, facing them with a bemused look, her spellbinding sunglasses showy and sly like those of a teenaged girl pretending to be a movie star.

"Hello, gentlemen," she said, with all the ease in the world.

•

Typing for others is like having a silent woodpecker drilling a hole into your forehead. You are you, in a relatively new skirt that itches at the edges (it's wool and you're allergic), with a firm and historical love for words—Nancy Drew on the porch, *War and Peace* one winter—and you are you who has many of your *own* private thoughts about the ways of the world, and would perhaps jot them down yourself someday, or even say them out loud to a table full of cognac drinkers, but instead you are you who is polite and also, let's get down to basics, need to make a living, and so you are being paid to type the words of others. Of a lawyer named William Mauster. His words go through your head slow and sure, like a TV anchor's cue card:

> It is impossible for Lisa Box to accept this renewed settlement offer on the grounds that Stratosphere is in no position to offer Lisa Box any of the Customer Base, for Lisa Box has a right to all of it without exception. As previously discussed, it is our contention, indeed our conviction, that when Mr. Grogon established Stratosphere, a Beauty Kiosk company that follows the Lisa Box model in every relevant manner, he was grossly disregarding the Partnership Agreement dated September 17, 1994, and amended on December 1, 1994. In the intervening time period, Lisa

Box has lost a substantial percentage of its business, solely due to the actions of Stratosphere. We are not impressed by the powerful distinction between "mall" and "airport." We do not believe that your "Ongoing Beauty Package," with the Web site and the club membership and the monthly renewals, reflects an approach to the Upgrade of Women that is so entirely different from that which is offered by Lisa Box. These are details; they do not impress, nor do they change the heart of the matter.

As you well know, we furthermore contend that Mr. Grogon has personally gone out of his way to egregiously and most unfairly and slanderously disrupt the good reputation of Lisa Box.

And we consider the Stratosphere College Scholarship program a blatant slap in the face, as it were, to our charitable enterprise, Lisa's Lil' Sister.

It is for these reasons that we hereby reject this settlement offer, as well as any future offers that do not take seriously the financial ramifications of these most harmful and, indeed, morally despicable actions engaged in by Leo Grogon and his company, Stratosphere.

Please do not hesitate to call if you have any questions. Very truly yours, William Mauster, Esq.

Welcome to the mind of Bill.

Anyway, Winona thought, he was the best writer of the lot. His sentences flowed without a preponderance of unnecessary *pursuant tos* and *heretofores;* he had the ability to make even regular language seem frightening. In person, he was a genius of anger, capable of threats and comebacks Winona couldn't make in her wildest dreams, but on paper he just plowed through like a bulldozer, no frills or fancy language required. Winona swallowed Mauster's thoughts, succumbing to his rhythms and arguments, his adjectives and decisions (though sometimes

29

it struck her as a touch overdone, a little idea—*Give me money!*—becoming a page, one fellow snowing the other with the power of bully words). Her fingers tripped lightly over the plastic letters; she imagined a scene she could film in which the shapes on the computer screen could be mimicked, gestured toward, by the landscape out the window; she wondered what Jeremy had meant when he'd called earlier and said he had "an exciting idea."

"What's going on in there?" Rex whispered, coming up behind her.

"She's in with Bill and Umar."

"Ah-hah!"

"Ah-hah?"

"Isn't it bizarre? Some mysterious company calls out of nowhere and offers us tons of work. All we need to do is hire this blind frickin' lawyer?"

"Yeah? So maybe they need discretion. Blindness is the ultimate in that regard."

"I don't know. I don't know."

"Listen, it's fortuitous. You know Ron hasn't paid us in three months," Winona said. "We need money. I need food and water."

"Why do they have to involve us at all? Why not just work through her?"

"Because they need a whole team. That's what we are."

"Oh, sure, wc all go together when we go."

"Rex, you're paranoid. Go watch *It's a Wonderful Life* or something."

"Hey, I did watch *Terminator* this weekend. What more do you want?"

"Can't get better than that."

"Okay, smarty-pants. Where's my new employment agreement?"

"What agreement?"

"Haven't you looked in your in-box lately?"

"I look in my in-box all the time. The wood-grain pattern is astonishingly lovely."

She actually had two in-boxes, priority and regular. No one ever put anything in regular. (All right, there was one memo from January 9 with *HOLD* scrawled in the corner.) Usually a lawyer didn't just drop a document in the priority in-box, he first rifled through what was already there, reorganizing a bit so all his work was on top. This shuffle of documents was politely ignored by Winona, who prided herself on impartiality. (Real priority never went in the boxes at all, but landed on Winona's chair or, sometimes, depending on the writer's anxiety level, precariously balanced on her keyboard.)

"You are a nutty downtown artist. And I suppose you're going to lunch now, too, leaving me and my work stranded, all alone, a sailor with no ship, no shore?"

"I'll do it, Rex, don't worry. When did you put it in?"

"Just now," he said, and gave her a foolish little grin.

•

Nancy set aside her project of refiling the firm's archival history in a color wheel of hanging folders.

She knew she was being naughty. She would only give herself fifteen minutes. Her room was infused with the swarming smell of the orchids. She tried to coax them with all the tricks she knew. She cajoled and murmured and willed them—and then there were the chemicals and the humidity hats and the lights and the temperature. That she never knew what would work made the process somehow delicious.

The aromas swirled in the room around her as she keyed in her password, and then the access code for the network.

It wasn't just prurient interest, although it had certainly come to that—Nancy realized this. She always knew she was in trouble when she didn't tell her husband about something. And over the years, more and more things like that had come up. In the old days, he was her confessor. She would tell him about the indiscretion or the selfish act, and she would be vulnerable and little, and he would be strong. He'd tell her the right thing to do. After a while, she didn't want to know the right thing to do anymore.

When they upgraded systems last year, the salesman had told her about this capability. She hadn't even thought about it until then, but he convinced her with statistics: research showed that in many major corporations, employees were logged on, writing or reading personal messages, visiting Web sites unrelated to work, for up to 20 percent of the work day. Twenty percent! It couldn't happen, not here, not where she was office manager. And to prove her sincerity to herself, she stopped using the system for her own personal business—and instead began reading the correspondence of her coworkers.

Rex was her favorite. She had no interest in him romantically, of course, but his correspondence held promise:

Hey Rex, I thought some more about what you were saying about your aunt who paints everyone porcelain animals for Christmas, and I thought, you're right, we have gotten so far away from all that. I just wanted to tell you that I went out and bought some yarn and I'm going to knit John a scarf for his birthday (not that he'll really want a scarf in May). Maybe it is true that the physical connects us to the real world. Well, I know you're out there looking for TRUE LOVE, but let me tell you that in the meantime you are bringing THE MEANING OF LIFE to lots of the rest of us, your pals. —Katy

What did that mean—true love? Nancy crossed her arms against her jacket, letting one hand trail underneath to the silk blouse. Professional women didn't wear fuzzy-wuzzy sweaters or organic cotton, they wore silk. Nancy felt the ridge of her bra beneath the creamy, shiny fabric. The strap was sharp and hard. She felt cold in her office, with Rex's e-mail on the screen, and then the screensaver came on, a field of stars that never stopped coming. It was a lonely screen, lonely and dark. The stars came at her but they never touched, they always drifted, careened, slid off the side of the screen, disappearing around her. Into the scent of the orchids. Into the sense that it was time to get back to work.

4 ✑

"WINOOONNNAAA!" erupted the Mauster monster. "Can you come in? With your pad."

Upon entering Bill's office, Winona always had the sense that she was in the midst of a ghostly clique of dreadful thinkers. A union of marble men sat cold, immobile, luminous—and in the face of such daunting stillness she had the perverse impulse to do a ballet step, to hop ahead with her arms extended and one leg stretched behind her. The stillness was everywhere. The miniature stock certificates, for example, seemed fluttery but were suspended in solid cubes of plastic. A little girl at the beach—a Mauster grandchild—was framed in a beveled silver square. The Hudson River, the Statue of Liberty, a weaving pigeon: all of New York City was rendered two-dimensional behind a plate of glass. Bill's coffee cup—

placed precariously now on a pad, half-on, half-off the desk—was the only glitch in the plan. It was the error woven into a carpet to keep the devil at bay, a potential for miracle, or disaster.

Though Bill didn't look up when Winona entered, she knew to sit down on one of the leather chairs facing his desk. She had her yellow pad with her.

Bill Mauster was reading a document, his elaborate fountain pen poised in his right hand, slightly trembling, gold tip gleaming, dot of ink alert to the imminent moment of possibility, of persuasion. He turned to the next page and read it, taking his pen to a certain paragraph, drawing a box around and a line through it, then writing a note in the corner. The silence in the sanctum sanctorum was broken only by the haughty scratch of his pen and Winona's irregular breathing. He turned to the next page. Winona gazed at his grandchild: a sweet girl, head full of curls, denim cap embroidered with flowers, little squirmy feet in the sand. Back to Bill's hand. A tremor in the pen, and now a stab forward: the unwanted word. Winona watched him create a long stretch of blue and a curlicue, the lovely dance of deletion. She sighed. This pause between fetch and follow-through was familiar. She looked out the window to the city, her home.

Winona had grown up in a little Cheever town in Connecticut, just an hour away, but the New York she knew then was Madison Square Garden, gleaming white, round-bellied Lippizaners dancing in a line, necks and heads bowed; fancy cats and their unsentimental owners at the cat show. It was the New York mapped out on the back of a grocery list by her mother, the loop between

Grand Central and the Museum of Natural History and back again, the stretch of Lexington Avenue where at fourteen she bought frosted lip gloss and purple nail polish from a store called Dazzle and platforms with burnished orange straps and five-inch wooden heels. Pretty soon it would be a city of rock concerts, Hank and Bruce and Mary and Lynn piled into a BMW and smoking pot and snorting coke, so much (for a tyro) that Winona bit through a plastic fork while eating spaghetti at the coffee shop before the show and that was hilarious and they hurried across Seventh Avenue to the Garden and got in after Neil Young had already begun, but what did it matter? This in itself was funny, was clever.

That was long ago. Now this was a new New York of burgeoning, wishy-washy intellectuals, young culture mavens, and impoverished, ever-hopeful artists. She'd come to the city to get her M.F.A. after a stint on the North Shore of Boston, working as a waitress, eating chocolate Häagen-Dazs out of five-gallon vats at the restaurant, staring out the window into quaint emptiness. Were the pilgrim ghosts bored, too? She'd moved to that little town with her then-boyfriend who managed an outdoor clothing store with gilt letters over the door and, inside, Patagonia whatnots and a basket of eyeglass holders. She herself was, as I mentioned, a filmmaker. Not a Hollywood filmmaker, God no, not even an artistic, experimental, underpaid filmmaker, the kind who doesn't have enough money (or possibly technical know-how) to make actual films, but who instead talks at parties about the superiority of black and white to color. No, Winona simply created scenes in her head. For instance, while swimming at the YMCA she envisioned an underwater camera that bobbed up and down like a swimmer doing the breast-stroke, up, down, up, down, in a slow rhythm, and on each downward bob the camera would gaze at the water-softened word at the end of the lane: *SHALLOW.* Then in a little flurry of commotion the swimmer-camera would turn around, and bob up, down, up, down, toward the other word: *DEEP.* Perhaps there would be a soundtrack, she'd thought—yes, amplified breathing, a steady, slightly exaggerated inhale and bubbly exhale, or some kind of stream-of-consciousness monologue on various subjects, shallow or deep, depending on your perspective. Her current idea involved a world where all the details were off. For instance, a character would go through an entire movie and each time any teenaged boy appeared in the camera he'd be carrying a huge SuperSip cup, one of those 36- or 48-ouncers. Nothing would be made of this, no close-ups, pauses, words—it would just be a world where all teenage boys constantly and forever drank out of massive cups. In this same movie, perhaps, the protagonist could misread things—a shampoo bottle in the shower would say *Nervous* instead of *Nexxus,* a votive candle would say *Carry me to bed* instead of *Carry me from this bedlam.* The entire world would be slightly confusing, but accepted without question, by the bathing, candle-lighting heroine.

Anyway, things didn't work out between Winona and that boyfriend (she didn't hike; she didn't wear Velcro or Tevas or that fake fleece crap), and it had been just about three years now since she'd moved to New York City to get on with her career as a non-filmmaking filmmaker.

Turns out, however, that with grad school and everything, the debts mounted (more than thirty thousand dollars in student loans) and even after she got her degree, no respectable jobs were forthcoming.

"I," Mauster began, turning to the last page in his document.

Winona snapped out of her reverie. The man with an *Esq.* at the end of his name, like an *e* on *old* or a bow on a hat, scribbled a sentence, sideways slanted, and set the document, at last, aside.

"I," he began again, drawing out the sound, "I would like you to turn your attention to the matter of a desk."

Now he was looking for something in the first few envelopes on the correspondence pile towering between the phone and the cigar cutter. A polite interval passed.

"What?" Winona asked.

"What?"

"A desk?"

"Yes, a desk."

"You mean, a desk for Sandy Spires."

"Of course," Bill said, taking his glasses off and looking at Winona. At times his eyes, which usually shone cold and ruthless, appeared almost warm, and Winona was reminded of snow shovels, winter nights, tartan jackets—a fatherly deal—and she wanted him on her side for a reason other than fear.

"I'll get right on it. It will be great to have her here."

He squinted at her, then put his glasses back on. "Yes," he said slowly. "Now I'll have more time to squeeze the life out of Leo."

Winona smiled politely. "Yes, I can imagine."

"Cretin. We're going to serve him his own balls for breakfast."

"No doubt."

"Now, I've got a few letters. The first is to Blane Rasmussen. Dear Blane . . ."

Winona scribbled. She didn't know shorthand. She wrote the first few words of each recited sentence faithfully, drawing a line for the rest.

Everything didn't feel exactly right, but then again, why should it? Winona had achieved, like a good air vent, climate control, a comfortable state in which the powers that be could barely touch her. In a sense she wasn't really there at all.

This situation would make Sandy's job easier.

•

The brochure was purple, no doubt the color of passion. Was passion all there was for couples? Surely that was, or might easily be, part of it. The first letters of both *Couples* and *Conference* leaped off the top like bunny ears. Embossed around the edges, in a circular cat-chasing-his-tail pattern, were the words: *joy contentment satisfaction vibrancy dialogue adventure humor passion forgiveness growth change enrichment security love.* Winona had to turn her head this way and that to get at all the meaning.

"So, I know what you're thinking. It's hokey. And it is. You're right. But you know, I've never tried anything like this myself, and it's not like I think we have any problems, per se, but just to get off on the right foot, you know what I'm saying?"

Jeremy looked hopeful, clutching a mug of green tea.

"But we're already off on a foot."

"Well, yes, but we've only taken one step. This will help us get to where we are going."

"What if this becomes where we're going?" Winona asked morosely. "What if we become the kind of people who go to couples' conferences?"

"We can do it once, big deal, see what it's like. The thing is, Winona, and this is important, you are important enough to me that I'd like to—I'd like to—"

He had trouble here. He wasn't the kind of guy who would tell you something just to get you into bed or what have you. If Jeremy complimented you, he meant it. He never used words loosely. Or indiscriminately. Or without an exquisite self-consciousness.

"I'd like to give it a chance," he said.

Jeremy had beautiful eyes, but so did all boyfriends when you were in love with them. Think of one boyfriend you've had who didn't have beautiful eyes. And Winona wasn't even in love, yet Jeremy held her hand when they were walking together down the street, and the first time they did that they had a conversation about whether they preferred all the fingers together or all the fingers splayed for the clasp, and he was okay with the way she liked it, splayed, and things just went from there, like dominoes. Or soldiers.

"I'd like to give it—us—a chance, too," Winona said, and reached for Jeremy's hand, "but, yuck! A 'workshop' on 'intimacy issues?'"

"I know, I know."

"Are you sure you're not just avoiding Mr. Williams?" Every once in a while he did garner obsessions that kept him away from his doctoral thesis for weeks at a time.

Once it was cleaning his apartment, really cleaning it, and selling off his old books. Once it was Tibetan chanting or something that required the purchase of woven straw mats.

"I'm sure," he said.

"Jesus, but it's a lot of money, too."

"I know, but it's worth it. It's love. It's our future."

Jeremy had not at this point told Winona he loved her, nor had she told him that she loved him. Now she speculated that he was using the term *love* in the catholic sense. Or in the manner of the candy heart.

"All right, sure. Two weeks. Be there or be single," she said.

"You are so sweet," said Jeremy, clasping her hand between both of his.

That night in bed—oh, never mind.

·

After reviewing the firm's monthly accounts with Bill later that week, Umar staggered up to Winona and leaned on the wall like the drunk's horse in *Cat Ballou*.

"Winona, we've got to collect some of this. Why hasn't Dr. Wellington paid this month? Christ! He's just playing with us. Just playing. Ron Blitzen—oh, God, just don't even bother. It's fucking ridiculous. Now, Jacketts and Rinaldi, they've got to pay up! These balances—we've been carrying them for months. A minimum payment, a monthly payment. Tell BonPizza we need a certified check by messenger or they can kiss their sorry-ass franchise good-bye. Darling, darling, *darling* Winona— you of all people keep this office in order. Please get these people to send us some money? Please? Pretty please? We're going to be ruined; the whole house of cards will come tumbling down. No more views, no more lunches—"

"No more ties from Barney's. I won't be able to buy that little Subaru I've had my eye on. The dishwasher on layaway will be lost," Winona chimed in.

"Exactly. You know everything. God, I have a headache."

"Too much excitement last night?"

"Oh, no, never. It's these early-morning shocks."

As Umar spoke, he gestured with his arms and tossed his hair back and forth. His suit was a subtle Italian pinstripe, his shirt silvery gray with those collars that said wealth, said excellent starch, and his tie was polka dotted. Yet he always had a ruffled look, as if he had just come in from some hotel-based interlude with a hot-blooded stranger.

"I've got some Tylenol, or ibuprofen."

"Maybe I should take some Tylenol. Or is ibuprofen better for a headache?"

"Well, it depends. I prefer Tylenol myself."

"No, no—I shouldn't take any. It'll upset my stomach. I'll just persevere."

"Okay," said Winona. "But Umar, shouldn't our retainer from Palm Consulting be coming in?"

She never seriously considered the possibility that the money would stop flowing at Grecko Mauster Crill: as long as these thick lawyerly walls were up, by God, she'd get her paycheck. Still, it was polite to play along with his distress.

"Yes, but we'll also have Sandy's fee. That's a new expense, and a big one at that. If fucking Ron would just get *himself* Upgraded, then we'd be in real business."

"Umar," Winona said. "I know it's none of my business, but listen. Since Ron's so poor right now, couldn't he just suspend operations at Lisa's Lil' Sister temporarily? Until Lisa Box gets back on track."

Much touted in the Lisa Box brochure, Lisa's Lil' Sister's mission was to fund reconstructive surgery for poor kids in third-world countries. Out of every one hundred dollars spent at Lisa Box, the brochure said, 10 percent went toward Lisa's Lil' Sister. This encouraged socially conscious women to go ahead and get Upgraded, for the benefit of all, and it made the company look good in the larger public eye, as well. Most of all, of course, it benefited the children. Reconstruction of cleft palates, separation of webbed fingers, skin grafts for burn victims—these were some of the most popular treatments.

"Can't do that, Winona. Lisa's Lil' Sister has a whole different charter. He couldn't raid it if he wanted to." Umar looked down at Winona sternly.

"Oh, okay. Well, anyway, everything should work out, it really should."

"Sure it will," he said, holding his forehead, making his way back down the hall.

Winona reluctantly pressed the PAST DUE stamp onto the bottom corners of this month's bills. The red was so garish! She was sure these people had their reasons.

•

Liz called later.

"I need a favor, sweetie. Could you *possibly* watch Sniffles for a couple of days—next weekend?"

"*Next* weekend?"

"Yeah—late notice, sweetie, I understand if you can't do it. Just let me know."

Her sister's voice had taken on that uncertain register where the words didn't match the emotion.

Liz lived in a tallish, prewar apartment building on East Twenty-fifth Street. Sniffles, a schnauzer, had suffered from runny eyes as a puppy. It was a "better" apartment, after all—Liz was a marketing manager at a credit card company—it just wasn't Winona's. Though she seemed to spend more and more time there. With Sniffles, the well-trained schnauzer.

"Sure, Liz."

"Oh, thank you! *Thank* you."

Winona hung up and rehearsed a call to Dr. Wellington regarding his bill: *Hello, Dr. Wellington? We need a little cashola around here? Either that or I'm going to come break your legs? Sir?*

Maybe she'd e-mail him; yes, that seemed like a better idea.

Besides the matter of the bills, Winona had the choice of a blind person's desk (pine? mahogany? candy-striped?) to occupy her. And behind that was the disconcerting fact that she was going to a couples' conference. And that she was having dinner with Jeremy again that night. Here's a transcript of the previous night's phone conversation:

"Hi, Winona."

"Hi."

"Whatchya doin'?"

"Laundry."

"Really? I did mine last night."

"Oh."

"Great minds think alike."

"Yeah—huh."

(Silence.)

Winona, feeling guilty: "How's work?"

"Oh, okay, I guess. I told you about the bird's nest near my window? Well, it fell off the sill. I don't know if a cat got it or what."

"Wow, bummer."

"How was your day at work?"

"Oh, no birds there, either . . ."

"Listen, since I know you don't have to do your *laundry* anyway, want to go out to dinner tomorrow night?"

"Sure," she answered—just like that.

"Great!"

The quiet door cracked open, and in came a little flurry of guilt. Who was she to judge, to find him boring? Besides, they were *coupling,* a new verb she had learned from the purple brochure. *(When two people couple . . . after you have coupled to your satisfaction . . .)* And so came the easy *Sure,* and, upon hanging up the phone, panic and depression.

She didn't exactly have a boatload of friends, either. Most of her classmates had gone West; some had become beyond-belief insufferable careerists. And there was no non-filmmaking filmmaker bowling league, or neighborhood association, or chat group on a friendly bench. There was, at least, an identity, the sanity of identity, in her normal work (if you could call Grecko Mauster Crill normal). But besides that, a person did need, at times, company.

From under a manila folder she pulled out the latest issue of *The New Yorker.*

She *was* a pretty good secretary, certainly, and this knowledge alone was sometimes a balm to her. She could type very fast, and she proofread with obsessive-compulsive zeal, and whenever she talked to clients she was nice and helpful. But she preferred to work in fierce bursts of all-out activity, leaving stretches of time for reading. She had stashes of magazines—by her desk, by the photocopier. She read whenever she could. The worse her day was, the more urgent her need to pick up a magazine. You could say she hid there, in the words, an escape within an escape: the magazines were a trapdoor.

That day she had developed an intense interest in bats, thanks to this astonishingly long article. A cave down in Arizona was once home to thirty million at a shot, yet they still had a very close family structure, and traditions—they all swirled around in a frantic dinnertime dance at dark, bat mouths pursed in a whistle, each child, teenager, dad, and grandmother whooshing through the air in Superman capes while the meatloaf bubbled over and green beans leached their color into boiling water. They lived in the same bat colony (on the same bat channel) forever. They were half one thing and half another, neither bird nor mouse but a disconcerting mix, like a novella.

It would behoove anyone to be called an old bat. Looks don't matter much for bats, so wisdom is everything—that and the continuing ability to spin around the air like a crazy person and to span two cultures, mammalian and avian. How old is an old bat? Old as her grandmother? Her mother? (Men were never old bats—pity for them.) If her mother were a bat, she'd be a department-store bat, bright and cheerful. Flying up the toiletries aisle, spinning through the spring shoe selection, nose diving between the racks of 50/50 blouses, pastel socks, and gold-plated trinkets.

There was something touching about these bat colonies, and Winona couldn't help but think of them as a little like a law office, like Grecko Mauster Crill, a portrait of the patriarch at the cave's center. She read to the end of the article, half thinking Bill's door would open or Umar would return and she'd have to slip the magazine under the desk blotter. Whenever the phone rang more than twice Winona picked it up. (Two rings meant the receptionist, Lucy, was either away from her desk or on the other line.) "Good afternoon, Grecko Mauster Crill?"— eyes scanning the row of vigorously discreet ads on the thin, shiny page of intellect.

There was a new element Winona wanted to put in her screenplay. The heroine could be driving along, and would come to a road sign where the words were out of whack, size-wise, so that a simple message, *passing CURVES right*, would confuse her merely from emphasis.

5 ⌒

MEMORANDUM

    TO: Grecko Mauster Crill Employees
FROM: Nancy Hobbs, Office Manager
    RE: New Associate!

We are pleased and honored to welcome Sandy Spires,
Esq., to the firm. Beginning on Monday, February 28,
Ms. Spires will be situated in the conference room, working on various projects with Mr. Mauster. Please make a
special effort to push your chairs in under the conference
table, and do not leave any stray objects in the hall.

Under the beneficent but murky gaze of Anthony
Grecko, Lucy Cummings changed from sneakers to
medium-high gold pumps, dropping her sneakers in a
massive black bag.

"Are they going to fire me?" she asked Winona as she
rummaged around, finally finding her High Floral makeup

48

kit. Lucy was always talking like that; maybe it was her way of making light of the fact that she was not only Grecko Mauster Crill's only black employee, but the only nonwhite person to be seen, except for delivery and house-keeping, on the entire 58th floor. She was the mother of a six-year-old, the much-loved Denzel, and though Bill and Nancy ostensibly had spouses, it seemed that Lucy was the only one with a hearth at home. She made lasagna on Sundays, went to church, and had a laugh that could ease even fat-cat lawyers. Now she adjusted her bra and opened her compact.

"I'll never let them fire you," Winona said.

"As if you have any power, but thanks anyway. Man, I need to start the day *over,*" Lucy continued, looking at her eyes and lips in the little mirror. "That's what I need to do. Just go back to six in the morning and start the whole thing over."

Lucy's hair was pressed and curled into ringlets, held back from her face with a wide black band. She primped, shook her head in private exasperation, snapped the compact shut.

"I'd start my day over in Paris, or Hawaii," Winona offered.

"Sounds great. I tell you what, there's a little boy in this world who literally chewed a hole in his Darth Vader cup, spilling grape juice all over Mommy's work outfit. The one she was going to wear to start the week off right, you know? Get to work on time?"

"Yeah, I know."

"So, do you think Mauster will let me go to parent-teacher day on Friday?"

"Sure, even he'd understand a thing like that."

"I don't know. He thinks of kids and insects as the same: underfoot, crunch when stepped on."

"Mauster? He likes kids!"

"Oh yeah, he loves kids. And I love lawyers," said Lucy, stuffing her purse underneath the desk and coming back up for air.

"He's got a photo of a kid right on his credenza."

"Uh-huh, and I've got pictures of lawyers in my head when I dream at night—so?"

"Actually, that kid may be himself; his inner child, I think," Winona mused, staring at Anthony Grecko—Tony, she called him.

"In drag. His inner child in drag. It figures."

"Everyone has to have a feminine side."

"Speaking of feminine, here comes Sharon Stone."

Winona turned around. Sandy Spires, in a red dress, opened the door and *tap-tapped* into the room. She wasn't alone. A handsome man turtle-walked in behind her, hunched around two boxes.

"Hello?" Sandy called.

"Hello," Winona and Lucy said at the same time.

"Ladies, good morning. I'm here to take over the empire."

"Good plan," said Winona.

"So, I think Bill said I'd be working in the back? The conference room?"

"Yes. I'll show you. Follow me."

"Great, Winona. Thanks. And Teddy's here to help me set up."

Sandy was standing still, the long white rod held lightly to the side, at ease.

"Hi, Teddy."

He was all muscle, a cheesecake cowboy type. Clearly ready and willing to do anything for this beautiful woman. Everyone needs a Teddy, thought Winona.

•

Winona had picked out a simple desk unit in cherry to go with the conference table and bookcases. It fit nicely between the window and the glassed-in bookcase with the more picturesque law books, and it had an extra shelf for Sandy's braille printer and scanner. Umar had put a second phone in, and they'd hired an electrician to install another outlet. In a home designer's flourish, Winona had adorned the top shelf with a glass vase of rose and green paper flowers. After Teddy left, Sandy stood before her desk. She reached forward and almost embraced it, then patted it down, as if she were a security officer and it a wayward tourist.

"It will be fine. I can use the conference table as well if I need to."

Her stark, ringless hands trailed up the sides of the unit.

"What's this?" she said, clasping the vase.

"Oh, flowers—decoration."

Sandy hesitated. "Well, okay. Very nice," she said. Then she reached toward the back of the desk. Lined up by the wall were three plastic cups: square, round, and triangular.

"And these?"

"Those? Those are pen holders," Winona said, rather pleased with herself. "They're different shapes in case you want to put blue in one and—"

Sandy started laughing. "Winona. That's—well, that's cute. Good initiative. But will you hate me if I ask you to take them back? You see, I can't actually stand clutter. And I don't use pens that often. Especially colored ones."

Sandy gathered the three cups in her hands and returned them to Winona.

"Oh, okay. I'm sorry—it was stupid of me."

"No, don't go that far. Here's a tip, Winona. No matter what, no matter how obvious the evidence in the other direction, never call your own ideas stupid. Okay?"

"Okay."

Unnerved, Winona tossed the cups through the Mr. Ed window to her chair and started the office tour. She showed Sandy the water fountain, right by the conference room door, and Bill's office at the corner of the main hall. Umar wasn't in so they walked on.

Step, step, *tap, tap.*

"And this is Rex's office. You met Rex before, I think?"

Rex got up from his chair and with a jovial seesaw gait made his way toward them.

"Hi, Sandy, how's it going today? Winona giving you the grand tour?"

He put his right hand out and with the left lightly touched Sandy's arm. They shook hands.

"She is. And Bill tells me you're going to give me some background on some of the firm's current business? The Lisa Box matter?"

"Oh, yes, I'll share all the sordid details, no holds

barred. Or is it bars held? I could never tell with that one. Anyway, before you can blink, you'll know everything there is to know about this godforsaken nuthouse."

"Looking forward to it."

Winona raised an eyebrow at Rex on her way out, then led Sandy farther down the hall.

"Nancy?"

"Yes!" Nancy got up quickly, as if she'd been waiting for them. "Hello, Sandy. I usually give the new employee tours, but we thought we'd give Winona a chance today. Is everything going nicely so far?"

"Yes, fine. Everything is fine."

Nancy looked at Sandy as if she were a threat to the natural order of things. It *was* true that Sandy had showed up on her first day in a red dress, like the exclamation point at the end of an unknown word.

"Well, good. Goodgoodgood. Has Winona given you the office manual? Oh, for gosh sakes," Nancy stopped. "You can't—"

"Give it to me on a disk or send it in an e-mail. My computer can read everything, and if I can't get it electronically we can scan it. What's that smell?"

"Oh, that?" Nancy laughed, a huge, relieved gust. "Those are my orchids. Not the flowers, you understand—most of these blossoms have almost no scent at all—but the leaves, the plant itself, the soil! They are splendid colors, pink, white, yellow—"

"Faultily faultless, icily regular, splendidly null, / Dead perfection, no more."

"What?"

"It's Tennyson. I majored in English, undergrad."

"Oh, poetry! How fun. My niece has some magnetic poetry on her refrigerator. Do you know magnetic poetry? Now *that's* fun."

"I don't doubt it, do you, Winona?"

"Certainly not, Sandy," Winona said, feeling once again nominally in control. "Shall we go on?"

They proceeded down the hall.

•

In the days to come, Winona listened to Sandy working in the next room. The blind woman used headphones to hear what she wrote, or what she was reading. The machine made some kind of accelerating hiss—but then there was also Sandy's breathing. She breathed heavily when she wore the headphones, as if mouthing the words as they came to her, sometimes sliding from breathing to whispering to actual speech. *Nonetheless, from the perspective of a jury,* she might say, and then trail back into a murmur. This oral letter-writing set Winona on edge, and she couldn't concentrate on her own work. She'd find herself holding her breath, waiting for the next word, wondering what secrets lay there.

It's the type of thing she could use in *The Anxiety of Everyday Objects,* Winona began to think. She wanted to use a soundtrack, that was certain; there was something seductive and intimate about information that came through the ear. But then again, perhaps she could make the same statement visually, through visual repetition. What was the difference, for the soul? Is there a difference between what you hear and what you see, or are they comparable, an aria to a sun collapsing over a French hill,

Lennon's "Instant Karma" to your hand stretched out a VW window, taking on the wind? Winona closed her eyes, opened them again. Sandy would never be able to answer such a question.

On the document holder, a transparent-blue ruler clasped yellow pages to metal; Winona went back to typing. *The third and perhaps most important point originates within your client's motivations themselves. What was he thinking when he paused for those five minutes, in front of the premises, after the accident had indeed occurred?*

"Hi," Rex said softly, leaning in the Mr. Ed window.

"She's got her earphones on," Winona whispered back.

"Double jeopardy."

"See no evil, hear no evil."

"You're naughty."

"Definitely not naughty enough," Winona answered.

"We met together, as you know."

"Yes—how was it?"

"It was okay. A little strange. She's a trip. Did you ever see *Kiss of the Spider Woman?*"

"She reminds you of John Hurt?"

"It's the eyes. Oh—sorry."

"Didn't you ever hear the phrase 'politically correct?'"

"Sure, it's what people without their own ethical center adhere to, like dressing for the weather. I have the moral precept of a boulder. You don't see a boulder putting on a raincoat, do you? It just takes it. And sunshine, too. I'm a boulder."

"Huh? What? You're exactly like a boulder, knucklehead."

"It's too early in our relationship to descend into petty name-calling. We don't want to form a precedent for the future—do we?"

"No, let's just be good to each other in the future."

"Okay."

"Phew."

"So, how's your sister?"

"She's fine."

"What did she do this time?"

"Nothing. Nothing at all."

"Did she go over the line?"

"She lives over the line. Just that sometimes I try to drag her back—usually without success. That's when the shit hits the fan."

"You are a brave, noble soul."

"Just kind of pathetic, as it turns out."

"Well, in any case, would your brave and/or pathetic self . . . would *you* like to go out—out to dinner—sometime, maybe this weekend? With me."

Winona stopped fiddling with the top of her paper clip holder. It seemed like a casual moment. They were still in their normal places: Rex hanging in the window, leaning on one elbow; Winona cross-legged in her secretary outfit—long skirt, pretty blouse, nylons, black pumps hovering between sensible and sexy. It was always the nylons she hated the most. They epitomized the entire experience: vaguely uncomfortable (but you got used to it), in a color one shade off life itself, outwardly smooth but filled with private difficulty (the way your big toe poked out of an ever-widening snare). She could answer this question better if her legs were bare. He was her friend at work, her funny confidant. And yet she was an artist, and it would be wrong, truly wrong, to go out with a lawyer.

"Sure."

"Okay, great!" he said, then slapped the sill, as abrupt as if he'd been hunting a mosquito that just landed there.

"Friday?"

"Yes!"

He slapped the sill again.

"Great!" he said, and was gone.

Winona resumed typing out of habit. Then she stopped and sat, staring at the screensaver. She hastily jiggled the mouse to get back to the document, but she didn't move for some time after that. Rex? Friday? She supposed there was nothing *too* wrong with one chummy dinner.

6

Winona sat on the futon couch and gazed at her sister's paintings while Liz finished packing in the other room, yelling questions Winona could neither hear nor (upon repetition) answer. Liz had just taken up painting recently. She used Windsor & Newton oils and prestretched canvas. She quickly, vibrantly framed the finished pieces (not holding with the idea that oil paintings should not be behind glass at all). The paintings were actually assignments from her Saturday afternoon class at the New School: still life with blue pitcher and white bowl, body part from live model (arm), landscape (from a photograph, a hammock-in-a-grove scene from Liz's trip to Bermuda), portrait (a pencil sketch, or perhaps it was charcoal, of—oh dear—a certain schnauzer), another still life, with lemons this time.

Liz had developed and undeveloped a few hobbies over the years, for edification, perhaps, but also to "meet other singles through your own interests." Tennis, wine-tasting, books. (Alas, the reading group was comprised only of women.) Liz often proclaimed that she was off men and that "men were from Mars anyway," but none-theless she persevered. The intensity of her search was fearsome at times; she engaged in it so seriously that it seemed the goal was not softly romantic but indeed rather alarming, and could possibly involve blood and armor.

"Winona, do you think polka dots are at all appropri-ate for a formal? Oh, you wouldn't know, for God's sake," Liz yelled from the bedroom.

The two yellowish shapes existed in a flat, expres-sionless universe, as if glued to a gray wall. The one in front had a provocative little nub, like a nipple, really, though fairly symmetrical, perhaps too symmetrical for nature?

"I thought this was a country weekend."

Liz snorted. Clatter of eyeliner or mascara on the counter.

"Well, it's not a hoedown, Winona. These are very civilized people. It's a *horse* farm. In fact, they're fucking millionaires."

"Polka dots are fine."

"Thanks. Dammit!"

"What?"

"My lipstick doesn't match this scarf at all."

Eventually Liz returned to the living room, hauling her suitcase in and then stuffing the side pouches with various articles: map, makeup case, umbrella. Sniffles stared balefully at the proceedings from underneath the cocktail table. Winona hadn't so much as scratched his head since she'd gotten there, nor had he paid attention to her. He always viewed Winona's arrival with fleeting delight, then dismay as he realized that her presence probably meant what it so often did—the absence of Liz. This feeling quickly degenerated into lie-under-the-table grade depression.

"When will you be home Sunday?"

"I don't know. Late afternoon, early evening."

"Can you be more specific?"

"Not really, Winona. Why, do you have a hot date or something?"

"Just want to know when I can go home is all."

Liz stood with her arms folded. Just two years her sister's senior, she had a polished look that made her seem rather older. Today she wore a blue-and-white Talbot's-type outfit: a white button-down blouse, blue jodphuresque pants, a blue cardigan, green socks dotted with blue bows, and slim black loafers. Her face was carefully made up, nothing distasteful about it, and Winona got a whiff of her perfume, Shalimar. It was the same kind their mother wore. Around her neck, Liz wore a red silk scarf in a jaunty if slightly outmoded side knot.

Sniffles came out from under the table then, and, in a dramatic turn toward denial, leaped toward his owner, as if they were about to go on a walk together.

"NO!" she shouted, and the dog skulked back toward, though not under, the table. He sat, woefully waiting for what might come next.

"Now, if you have a chance, the recycling is completely full. I meant to get to it before I left, but I didn't.

Also, if I get any calls at all, can you *please* have them leave a voice message? It's so much more convenient than written messages. And try not to stay on the phone forever. For some reason call waiting doesn't work with the fax number, and Bettina said she'd be faxing me the info on Laurie's shower."

"I thought I'd have a keg party tomorrow night. I'll leave you what's in the keg and any leftover pork rinds," Winona said.

Winona's job was to do her sister's bidding. It had been this way since she was old enough to stumble about their bedroom, playing baby princess to the mommy princess that was Liz. Winona didn't particularly resent the work; actually, she sort of liked it. The role wasn't particularly challenging. It was comfortable. She was used to it. Teasing her sister was the perk.

This time, Liz ignored the taunt.

"There should be enough food for Sniffles, but if not, just get some and I'll reimburse you, of course. It's Hill's Canine W/D—*nothing else.* You've got to get it at Dr. Thompson's, on Twenty-third and Lex. Sniffles really likes to be walked three times a day, not just two anymore. So if you have a chance . . . but I wouldn't want to impose. I mean if you have anything planned or anything . . . Do you?"

"Just the keg party."

"Oh, be serious. I've *got* to get out of here."

"No, I don't have any plans," Winona said.

"Okay. You hear that, Sniffles? You're going to get some TLC this weekend. Poor little wittle-ittle."

Liz leaned down and gave him a dramatic air hug and kiss, as if she were already at a society ball.

"Win, sweetie, thank you *so* much, you're a *doll*. Have a great weekend!"

"You, too, Liz. Remember, withers are in the back of the boat. You steer with the forelock."

"You're so silly!" Liz had gotten cheerful now that she was wheeling her suitcase toward the door. "There's some leftover Virginia ham in the refrigerator! Bye! Bye, Sniffles!"

When Liz was gone, Winona groaned and lay down on the couch, legs hanging off the side like she was a Raggedy Ann doll. A mile away—a Manhattan mile, which are the longest miles in the world—a black-and-white cat sat in a studio apartment, hoping at least for a cockroach to add spark to the lonely hours. Winona and Sniffles remained silent in Liz's living room for a few minutes, their eyes closed. Finally, they faced each other.

"Well, Sniffles. Are you ready to meet the Rexmeister?"

•

Winona took a shower. Not for Rex's sake, God knows— they wouldn't be *that* close to each other. She just wanted to feel new and alert, though in truth there was something fun about dressing for a date, even if it was a non-date such as this one. There really couldn't be less of a *date* date than this—it was almost a reverse date, an etad. Still, she used Liz's Japanese-French bath gel, slip-smoothing it around her shoulders and arms and stomach. Standing naked, toothbrush in her mouth, she rifled through Liz's closet—the best part of staying there, that and the ninety-two cable channels—and came upon a dark blue, almost black, silk blouse that would look nice with jeans, and now all she needed was the right belt.

She'd wear her white-and brown-armadillo cowboy boots. She cursed because she *had* the right belt, at home. All her sister had were stupid-ass belts. (Belts are faster arbiters of fashion than blouses, almost as fast as shoes.) So she'd wear her jeans without a belt. She sprayed her neck and wrists with her other perfume, her come-closer elixir, and dried her hair, flipping it from side to side, flip, flip, like Peppermint Patty and the dancing girls.

That Rex was actually going to meet her here was an unpleasant truth, making the evening seem more formal than she wanted, more man-woman. (It was Jeremy the Sincere's *lack* of picking her up for dates that bothered her there, but anyway.) Thankfully it would be man-woman-dog, and that took some of the pressure off. Sniffles could break the ice.

●

"Hello, Win," he said when she opened the door. He was wearing jeans and a dark green pullover. She was taken with the way he looked; she'd never seen him out of a suit before. But was Rex ill at ease? She wasn't sure. She'd never get through the evening if *he* were nervous.

"Hi! This is Sniffles."

Rex looked down at the yapper. "Yo, Sniffles."

"Come in," Winona continued. "I should tell you the package went out—Saturday delivery."

"Of course it did, I wouldn't doubt you for a second."

She looked at him suspiciously. They walked to the living room.

"So, this is where Liz hatches her visions of grandeur?"

"Yup."

"Those are nice paintings."

Winona lifted her eyebrows, then turned to look at the wall with the art.

"She painted them."

"Really?"

"She'd like to know they were admired, yet on the other hand if I tell her you were here she'll think the worst of both of us."

"They show a kind of integrity of purpose. A unique way of looking at things—not your typical marketing manager scheme, those lemons."

"Intriguing, Rex. Look, you can see the top of our building from here."

Rex walked up to the window, hands in pockets. He peered out to the side.

"Is that Mauster? What's he doing with that—that kite! Bill is flying a kite out the window, Winona. See that?"

"You're a laugh and a half," Winona said, snapping back the curtain.

7 ∽

Any outsider would think they made an attractive couple, that perhaps they were, in an odd, unquestioned way, absolutely right for each other. They *looked* easy enough as they walked the few blocks down to Café Joie de Vie, recommended by a friend of Rex's who lived nearby. They were young and happy and kind of bouncy, both of them, as if they were going someplace they wanted to be. There was a moment there, on the street, when they could have just handed over their IDs to some uniformed delegate and entered a new world, where all that they were wasn't already fixed, where ties and pantyhose and reactions and counterreactions could be dropped at the door.

When they got to the restaurant, Winona discovered it was nice, a *nice* restaurant, and this once again made her nervous. It was a real-flower-in-the-wee-vase joint. They had a young, pretty server named Heather.

"Do you want to see a wine list?" Heather asked.

"No," said Winona.

"Yes," said Rex, then looked at Winona. When Heather left, he asked, "No wine for you?"

"Oh sure, wine. We could have wine. Maybe they have a carafe."

"Or better yet, a bowl."

"A bowl?"

"Maybe something homemade, juniper berries and Welch's jelly."

"I should remember not to trust your judgment with the client base."

"Hey, I can be *very* clearheaded. It's Friday, though, so I want to be an artist, like your friends—bohemians, intellectuals, Marxist leaders."

"I don't have any friends."

"Oh, reassuring."

They looked at their menus. *This is going to be a perfect fiasco,* Winona was thinking. *I hope we don't mess up our work relationship. Try to remember the humor in the situation. Lighten up. Enjoy dinner. Concentrate on the small things you have in common.*

"Is it that you want to have sex?" Winona asked, temporarily putting off the decision between steak and trout.

"What?"

"Well, I mean, is that what dating is all about? This seems like a date."

The words had jumped out without her consent. Now she felt like she had ruined something, everything.

"Winona, I don't want to talk about how attractive I find you. It's my secret."

"Oh."

They looked back down at their menus. Winona contemplated an escape through the bathroom window. Rex put his menu aside again and leaned forward.

"May I buy us a nice bottle of wine tonight? I don't know what any of these are, but if I just go for high price, and toss in a little sophisticated French, I should be all right. But only if you'll let me."

She shrugged, what the hell? "Okay, I'll have some wine. Some nice wine. The best."

"Good. Now we're getting somewhere. And after dinner, do you think we should quit our jobs? For fun? Do you think we would ever have met without Grecko Mauster Crill?"

"I don't know, what does 'meeting' mean?" Winona continued rather gloomily. "People meet all the time and they may as well be wallpaper to each other."

"I don't know about that. Even the smallest meeting can be perfect. You can sit next to someone on the train and comment on the coldness of the chrome and chuckle together about the trainmaster and that's it, that's perfect. Or you can talk to someone about, say, *Casablanca* on a plane from New York to Chicago, and it can be the most heartfelt conversation in the world, and you will never see that person again, you don't even know her name, but it was still a perfect hour over beer and peanuts at thirty-thousand feet. Or you can have a longer conversation, one that takes days, weeks, years."

"Wow," said Winona.

Heather returned and Rex ordered not a French wine, as it turned out, but a pronounceable little number from California.

"The question is," Winona said, "who you are when and with whom. For instance, I'm sure there's one Winona to Mauster, another to my sister, and another, say, to you. They're not all the same Winona. If I told my sister the story of, for instance, the reason I moved from the second to third floor in my apartment building, and if I told you, and if I told Mauster (I wouldn't tell Mauster), then the story would change a little each time. So in a sense everyone 'meets' me, but in another way I am constantly shifting around as I meet them. See what I mean? But I think, to get back to it, maybe we wouldn't have met without Grecko Mauster Crill. But have we *really* met?"

"Yes, I think so, Winona. I do. Maybe we've *just* met. But tell me, why did you move to the third floor of your apartment building?"

"Oh, that's a long story."

"Heather isn't exactly light on her feet."

"Well, it was too noisy where I was, so I moved up a floor."

"That *is* a long story."

Winona laughed a little, half-forgetting her earlier faux pas. The waitress brought the wine.

"To you," Rex said.

"To you, too," said Winona, and they clinked glasses.

"Yum," she said.

"A distinctly yum character with a hint of woodsy yum in the background. So, we've got our basket of bread, a vat of butter. Wine. And you were telling me—upstairs, downstairs? The long story of the apartment?"

"I forgot."

"Okay, let me guess. The Three Stooges lived next door to you, and it was back when they were keeping a white horse in their apartment. It wasn't really a problem at first, but then they all got jobs on Wall Street, and they left the poor creature alone all day, and he'd whinny a sad whinnying song every day because he missed them so."

"Don't say that! You'll remind me of my cat, who is miserable and alone tonight as I drink delightful wine and later coddle the irredeemable Sniffles."

"Tell me, then."

"Okay, the situation was like this. I first got my apartment when I moved to the city. It was a dump and a slum, though I painted the walls a nice shade of peach. Anyway, it was always *my* dumpy slum, and I loved it. I was going to NYU then, studying film. Then my friend Wendy, who was also in the program, needed an apartment. I called my landlord, and lo and behold, there was an apartment opening up, the one next to mine. We were psyched! We were good friends, and even though we wouldn't have wanted to live together necessarily, living next door would be perfect—borrowing cups of sugar, giving fashion advice, having secret wall-tapping codes. It was good, pretty good, for a while. It was when I had a big crush on this guy, Joel, a soon-to-be-swaggering-director at school. I mean a really big crush. Probably one of the top three loves of my life."

"Top three, eh?"

"So the thing is we finally went out a few times. And it didn't really work out. It just didn't. And suddenly Wendy and Joel were dating. Dating, and then Joel was sleeping over at Wendy's almost all the time. And it was noisy. Very noisy. I moved upstairs to another apartment."

"That sounds pretty depressing."

"As it turned out, they broke up fairly quickly. But by then Wendy and I had lost something—or everything. Pretty soon she moved to Boston."

"Really? Well, where I live, things are a lot less exciting. Guys wear suits, no one lives together until after marriage. It's an uptown kind of thing."

Heather returned with their salads.

"Why do people go out to restaurants, do you think?" Winona asked as she detangled fennel from cucumber and laid it on the side of the plate. She wanted to create an even pile but couldn't get the fronds to cooperate.

"To eat?"

"Sometimes I get anxious in restaurants," Winona admitted.

"It's a whole pleasure thing, I think—the pleasure of sitting and eating dinner. Talking to someone you like."

"I often feel I should be enjoying myself more than I am."

"Perhaps it's simply been a case of the wrong vinaigrette."

"Possibly that's it."

"What about tonight?"

"Tonight?"

"Do you feel that way tonight?"

"No, actually. Not tonight," Winona said, going red; a spot of pepper had got stuck in her throat.

Soon their meals came: steak au poivre for her, mussels in wine sauce for him. He pulled off a hunk of bread and put it on his plate.

"So, I'm always fairly certain half or less of your brain is occupied at work with work. What in God's name do you think about, anyway?"

"I always have my mind a hundred percent on my job, Rex; you should know that. Sometimes, on a coffee break, I might think of *The Anxiety of Everyday Objects.*"

"The *what?*"

"That's my movie."

"What movie?"

"I'm writing a movie—*The Anxiety of Everyday Objects.*"

"What's it about?"

"Well, do you ever look at a sign and you think it says something different than it really does? Like the sign says TURN AHEAD and you read it as TURN AROUND, and you feel as if it's a personal message just for you?"

"Er—"

"Or you're in the subway and you keep seeing words on stray sections of newspapers, and all together a sentence is coming through word by word?"

"And the message is, 'You're the Son of Sam?' Or maybe 'Elvis is alive and well and living on East Twelfth Street?'"

"I'm hoping it's more subtle than that."

"Is it magic realism? Surrealism?"

"It doesn't have a name. That's part of the anxiety."

"Does your film have people in it?"

"Sure, there's the woman who sees it all."

"What does she do?"

"Sees things—that's the important part. She might have a job or something."

"A love interest?"

"No love interest."

"Oh. Too bad," said Rex, spearing an artichoke.

Later still he asked about her family, and she told him about her parents, who lived in Florida and played way too much golf to maintain any degree of sanity. They were good parents, or had been, but now they wore too much plaid and Kelly green. And pink visors. And tassled everything. Then he told her about *his* dad, he of the gold-rimmed glasses and a life devoted to law, and his mom and her sick mother, who lived with them for the years prior to the divorce, then died the week his father left. They both seemed shy after that.

"I wish there were rules for stuff like this," she said.

"Describing your parents? Or dinner conversation?"

"Both."

But there were not. Outside them, a world was always being built, always seeking order for itself. There were trains to get people where they wanted to go, some that headed far away, some that only went a short distance. Streetlights told certain travelers to halt, and others to go. There were multiple, well-marked places for buying everything necessary for warmth, hunger, thirst, adventure, lust, education, burial, birth. The kitchen trash went in a little white sack and then a green Dumpster and then a blue truck and then landed in a heap in some vast, untold wasteland. Food came from the same place, only on the other side of the hill, back to the city in another truck, in a crate, in a sack. People had figured out how to get electricity, and water came through a spigot, and there was this sense of a deep, strong order to all that had been done. And with the order came an unfamiliarity with the language of chaos—the chaos of weather, violence, survival, ingenuity, love, also inherent in all things, of course.

•

On the way back to Liz's apartment, Winona asked Rex if he'd like to walk Sniffles with her. It was a warm night, and the air had a velvetiness to it that was either romantic or the sign of unhealth. They walked slower now than their crazed half-gallop to the restaurant. Rex had taken her arm—"We can look more civilized than we are"—and Winona had realized that they were a good height for each other and she enjoyed, for the moment, the loop she was in, the neither rigid nor disinterested enclosure of his arm. At dinner, they had both leaned into the table, fork or glass or bread in hand, and spoke and listened with intensity, cheeks flushed, eyes flashing. Now, unconsciously, Winona leaned into Rex when they passed shambling figures asking for cash.

When they came back down the elevator with Sniffles, the dog was a gleaming, cartwheeling star of stupid delight. He shook his salt-and-pepper self, his hefty barrel belly. He scratched at imaginary fleas—the scratchy-itchy feeling dogs get from being cooped up in the city. He did what he needed to do and it was only after *that* that he remembered his disdain, his general irritation with the babysitter and this other one, this happy man. He gave them rueful looks over his shoulder, doubting them seriously when, at various junctures, they deviated from the route Liz, the good Liz, took every morning and evening.

She wasn't looking for a boyfriend, Winona told herself again. But when Rex looked at her with his gray-green eyes, she didn't know if she'd ever seen that color before, though she'd spent hours in conversation with him, and in better light. They walked up Lexington Avenue past an old Chinese restaurant with a red bowl in the window filled with dyed red plumes, and a circle of what seemed to be chips from a broken blue-and-white plate. Green and red neon from window signs swept over them like carnival hieroglyphics, and they approached the next in a series of easy decisions—red, green, yellow, don't walk, walk. Before they knew it they were crossing Thirty-fourth Street, and Sniffles had begun to lag, slack-leashed, and Winona was thinking about men's skin, how underneath the shave was a cloud of dark that reminded her of something, the woods maybe.

"That was before I went to college and realized that Marxism wasn't really the evil spawn of the devil, but it was a philosophy, a flawed philosophy, but a worldview nonetheless," he was saying. "Did you take philosophy in college?"

"Huh? What?"

He repeated the question.

"Oh, well, yes. No. I didn't take philosophy, I took English mostly, no math. Rex, let's turn around."

"Want to go back up Third?"

"Sure."

He steered her sideways. "Political science?"

"No."

"You were always a liberal arts type of girl, right?"

"In college I was a woman, it's only in recent years that I have become a girl again."

"And what's a girl, then?"

"A girl—" Winona began, intoxicated, perhaps, by the unlikely smell of lilac on this street. "A girl is a person on a trampoline, not her own trampoline, but the neighbor's. A girl is a person who laughs at things, and who might have a pink plastic umbrella. A girl would make sure that the pencils provided for the SATs were yellow and green and blue, and she'd never let them outlaw horse-drawn carriages."

"This is more complex than I thought."

Winona warmed to her subject. "A girl chooses to be a girl. It's not about making tuna casserole for the boys, or joining some bobby socks bowling league. And it's not really Cyndi Lauper or The Go-Go's, either, although they come closer."

"So a girl—a girl borrows trampolines?"

"A girl can do anything she wants. She can even be a waitress or a secretary, but she has to have fun while she's doing it. And if she wants, she's got to be willing to make a paper airplane out of her job description and sail it out the window. Above all, she's her own person. A free person, having fun. I guess that's the key to being a true girl."

"I am impressed with your definition and glad to know it. I wonder if there is an equivalent for boys—men—guys! If so, I'd like to be it. A true male whatchamacallit."

"I think you are just that. As it turns out. A true male whatchamacallit."

"Really? I'm honored."

They were back on Twenty-fifth.

It was as if she had driven up to the edge of a cliff and when she got there all the fragrant breezes of springtime in Big Sur—the eucalyptus and the salt and the grasses and the moon and the pine and the flowers—had disarmed her, shaken things up a bit. But still, she wasn't in a convertible in California, she was right here, and things were measured in square feet in New York, and she always rounded up, and she got her twenties out of machines, two, three times a day, and she went to work at nine and left at five-thirty, and she was almost thirty and she hadn't made her movie, and if she didn't watch out she'd get subsumed entirely into the world of law, of trench coats and bylaws, so she had to back up, back off, stay away, and so no, she wasn't really happy, she wasn't actually a free person, and so despite the speech she wasn't a girl after all, come to think of it, and so no sex for her, no flowers, no Big Sur, no springtime, and especially NO REX—with his little ears and his perfect manly hands and his annoyingly green-gray eyes.

"Well," she said, at the doorway.

"Well," he said back.

"I guess I better tell you that we should only be friends," she said in a rush.

He smiled. "I want to be friends, too, Winona. That's what I want."

What did he mean by that? In his eyes she saw only a gentle casual niceness, not a wimpy niceness, but a let-me-take-the-wheel-and-drive-us-through-the-rough-patch nice. But there was just no way. He was a lawyer. They worked together. And let's not forget Jeremy.

"Okay, well, thanks for a wonderful evening."

Rex squatted down and roughed up the dog's ears.

"Little pup, the lady has used the word *friend*, and I think she meant it in the most ominous way. You know which way I mean, don't you, Sniffles? So it's baseball and Don Miguel frozen burritos for me this season. All I can say is thank God for ESPN. But here—" he said, standing again, and pulling out a handful of André mints from his jacket pocket. "I got them for you at the restaurant."

"Thanks," Winona said, her hand full of green glint.

She watched him walk away, looking a trace jaunty. Sniffles watched, too, alert to the moment when small, pocket-originating treats were handed out, and feeling that there had been an opportunity missed, somehow, something he'd missed the whole night.

Art

In which Winona struggles with craft

1

Winona sat in the lobby of the Grand Hyatt with her pad, her pen. The room was a suffocating tropical hell. Someone versed in such things had created, in carefully positioned Nature Squares, great plumages of greenery and hissing fountains. Shadows with suitcases strode up to a counter manned by clerks in burgundy-and-gold uniforms. Whatever they said to each other was muted by a din, low and insistent like the reverberation of a drum outside the space-time continuum.

A handful of workers from adjacent office buildings came here on their lunch hours; Winona was one of them. A baggie, from which she had drawn out her peanut butter and jelly sandwich, was now empty and folded discreetly under her thigh. Diet Coke and peanut butter and jelly on whole wheat was perhaps the most ghastly combination known to mankind—yet what could she do? It was cheap; she had become accustomed to it. In a way, she liked how horrible it was, how horrible and effervescent.

As usual, Winona was trying to find a way into Anxiety, a way to represent it. Her page was blank.

If only she were one of the people who walked briskly on their lunch hour, or lifted barbells, or jumped around in giddy pink outfits with throngs of athletic others. If only she meditated, like Jeremy, or went to a self-help group (free, in a manner of speaking), or worked through her lunch, like the lawyers themselves, those who truly had a stake in the place.

Indeed, the lunch hour, which she yearned for and clung to, was perhaps the worst part of her day, the locus of meaninglessness in the secretary's world. Sixty minutes: the freedom was painful, and the brevity made it useless. What could she do in an hour? If there were a Lisa Box handy, she could make herself over, twice. (If you make yourself over twice, do you become who you once were?) Instead she tried, with limited success, to be herself.

But if she was herself only at lunch, who was she the rest of the time? Was she someone else? Were those, the majority of the hours, nothing? Or were they the truth?

Was she, in fact, a secretary above all else?

Who are you? I'm a secretary.

Perhaps also she was becoming more and more *that way* the more hours she spent at Grecko Mauster Crill— the you-are-what-you-eat theory. Surely there was a threshold. She could be a filmmaker only so long who never made films, who scratched out some notes here and there between vast swaths of secretary activity. At a certain point, didn't one override the other, create personality, fate?

At the office she was busy. Here, in the lobby of false tropical splendor, she crouched, pen to page, her head cheap and strung out on Nutrasweet, her legs swathed in nylons, her silly shoes placed politely beneath her knees.

No champion of the avant-garde ever looked this way.

•

"Where's Lucy?" Sandy Spires asked the next morning, handing a disk through the Mr. Ed window.

"I don't know, Sandy. She's usually here by nine or so," Winona said, taking the disk.

"It's nowhere near nine. It's nine-fifteen."

"It is."

"The call you just put through to me? That was the attorney general's office. They had tried a few minutes before, too, and there was no one here picking up the phone. I'd like to know why not?"

"I'm sorry. I must have been in the bathroom."

"Look, I know you can't always be at your desk, but isn't that why we have a receptionist? She's hired to sit in her chair and answer the phone from nine to five-thirty. It's not that difficult."

"Well, she's got a little boy and sometimes she has to—"

"Winona, do you think the attorney general cares about Lucy's personal problems?"

Today Sandy was wearing a steel-blue jacket made of some kind of Vietnamese silk, and a blouse underneath that seemed partly, alluringly, organic.

"I guess not," admitted Winona.

"But *you're* very responsible about time, aren't you?" Sandy now asked, changing her tone.

"I suppose," said Winona. She was on time only through extreme willpower. She wasn't late, nor did she take home Grecko Mauster Crill pens or make personal photocopies between memos of threat and understanding. On the surface this seems virtuous, but these forays into asceticism gave her days order, not joy.

"That's good in a secretary."

Winona smiled bleakly. Sandy seemed to be staring at the space directly above her head.

"And you've been here for . . . a year or so?"

"Yes, almost a year and a half."

"Did you go to school to become a secretary?"

Winona flushed. "Actually, I went to school *not* to become a secretary."

"I guess that didn't work out too well," Sandy said.

"No . . . liberal arts . . ."

"What did you say?"

"It was a liberal arts degree . . ." Winona mumbled.

"Well, to my understanding, you're more than a secretary here. You virtually run the place."

"I do?"

"Sure."

"Of course, Nancy is the office manager, and—"

"Nancy is writing cutesy memos. Nancy is watering her plants."

"Oh."

"You'll do fine, unless your mind atrophies in the meantime. You don't want to be like those kids in some city schools—they literally come out dumber than they go in."

"Well, I'm glad to be part of something larger, the common cause and all that. We've got a good team here, don't you think?"

Sandy's blackberry-bruise lips were raised now in a kind of smile. She tapped her fingers, nails chewed to the quick, on the windowsill.

"'A Good Team.' Sure. That's a nice way of looking at it. Anyway, Winona, I need you to draft a new promissory note for me, this is the amount." She recited a figure and Winona took it down on her pad. "That's from Lillian—with two *l*'s—and Andrew Rasmussen, to Blane Rasmussen."

"Sure, right away."

"You'll use the same template as we did for Dr. Wellington and his wife."

"Of course."

Winona watched Sandy walk back into the conference room, veer toward a chair, and right herself. Winona inserted the disk into her hard drive, pleased, though somewhat unsettled by, the compliment Sandy had given her.

•

The day after her friendly get-together with her friend Rex, Winona had gone back to her apartment to spend a few hours with Fruit Bat. When she got there, he had already knocked over her spider plant and eaten it all the way down, like a small mowed lawn. She fed him some muck out of a can, rubbed his ears, and sat on her bed with a cup of coffee and *The New Yorker* on her lap, unopened.

Perhaps she should put the heroine of *The Anxiety of Everyday Objects* in some kind of sensory deprivation site and make the whole movie a kind of paean to ordinary life—what she was missing, yet what she *continued* to miss because in her imagined ordinary world nothing was quite right, the way in a dream an airplane can also be a car and a train and a homeland.

The call had come in, the call that would go unanswered. She and Fruit Bat stared at the ringing phone and its attendant answering machine. "Hey, Winona," Rex said through the ether. She should get up, she should get up, she wasn't getting up, he was saying: "Just wanted to thank you for having dinner with me last night. It was fun. Looking forward to collating mortgages with you on Monday." *Click.* The machine clucked and spun and there was a little red *1* where the *0* had been.

Winona thought about Rex's gray-green eyes. Why hadn't she ever noticed them before? Would she notice them again? She would not.

Winona could not imagine any happy or useful action. But she felt sure of something new in the wake of her date with Rex, something that had come upon her as she had slept in Liz's bed with Sniffles last night, while Fruit Bat slept here, in her abandoned apartment: she had to break up with Jeremy.

The couples' conference was on Saturday. Her mother had once suggested that Winona break up with a certain other boyfriend after the holiday season ended; it was all about timing. Perhaps this was the same sort of thing? Go to the conference, share, heal, and then head for the door? It seemed wrong. Yet if she didn't go with him, what would he do? He had a ticket to spare.

It was time, really time, to be straightforward.

The Green Bee of Madagascar is a small creature with an extraordinarily high-pitched hum. Its wings are the briefest snippets of conversation; its stinger is shiny, long and curved like an enchantress's pointer finger. Instead of yellow and black stripes around its belly, it has an emerald-green body with an amazing red dot on the breast, as if it is the victim of a tragic love disaster. Its beady black eyes see things magnificently, or not at all. Through those bulbous, bubble-hard lenses everything is broken into parts of itself: the texture, the temperature, the scent, the illusion that holds the heart together.

Because of this little bee, all hell had recently broken loose. It seemed, first of all, that there was an unexplained potency and vigor to the male beekeepers back in Madagascar, and a cornucopia of fertility in the female beekeepers. The article even said that one beekeeper—her name was Lenora—got pregnant three times at once; she gave birth to a new kind of triplets. There was another case in which a male beekeeper imagined pressing his face between the breasts of a young girl in town (she was only 14), and without even touching her, without so much as a kiss or snuggle, she became impregnated by him, by his desire. There was lore, there were rumors: eggs swelling and pushing outward; a seminal fluid so sweet and sticky nothing could escape its path; twins and triplets frolicking in the clover and lupine hills. Women's legs were like Venus's-flytraps, sultrily, deliciously, murderously encompassing their lovers.

When this little bee found its way to the West, however, it brought a terrible epidemic bee flu, killing 80 percent of all the domestic bees in the U.S. No corresponding fertility was found in any of the American beekeepers, who were languishing in economic woe.

Winona stared at the small sketch of a man in a beekeeper hat accompanying *The Wall Street Journal*'s middle-column story of passion and strife. Over the beekeeper's head flew a fanciful bee. Was it the Green Bee of Madagascar, or just a lethargic, not-so-fertile American bumble buzzer? Winona took a sip of coffee and wondered.

2 ～

Nancy watched the red lights on the phone. Through her open door, she could hear Lucy on the phone, and in the time the hotel manager had kept her on hold, Nancy had felt the irresistible urge, like the need for a cigarette. She could dip in and out, perhaps. She looked back up at the door—no one was coming. But then the idiotic hotel manager got back on the phone.

"Is this for a meeting?" he asked.

"Yes."

"Right-o, so it's a meeting. How many people?"

"Five, as I said!"

"Do you want a hotel room with a suite, or a meeting room?"

"What are the benefits of a hotel room?"

"Well, you've got a shower, and a bed."

"No one will need to shower during this meeting," Nancy replied icily.

"Right-o. You can have one of our executive lounges—they come with a stocked refrigerator, microwave, ice machine, a/v capabilities including a full-sized video screen and monitor—"

"Fine. And for lunch, we need a reservation in your very best location."

"All areas at Lily's are very nice, ma'am."

Nancy huffed. "All right, fine," she said, getting off the phone with the insufferable man.

Umar passed by in the hall. Nancy waited just a minute, then she got up and quietly shut the door to her office. Instead of sitting back down, she stood by the windowsill, savoring the moment. The Lydias were looking lovely, red blossoms tangly and ragged and dripping delicately. Since the parasite problem, she'd been worried, but the wash seemed to have helped, and now they looked better than ever, better than last year. Nancy was pleased. She touched one of them with her fingertip, the false nail a shade more orange than the flower, and then she lightly touched the little white root that had pushed out of the soil and made its way toward the edge of the pot. *Tender little root, where are you going? You are going the wrong way. I'll chop you off if you misbehave. No, no. Of course I wouldn't do that to you, my dear flower.*

She turned back to her desk and sat before the computer.

Dear Katy, Rex had written, just this morning. I thought about what you said last night. I don't know if I should take your advice literally. Persevere? I'd like to, I told you that, but when a woman says "let's be friends," and then doesn't even answer your phone call, you've got to take it as a sign. I think Winona and I could easily be really right for each other, but it's got to be a two-way street. Who knows, I probably had a raddichio leaf hanging off my shirt collar half the night.

Nancy sat back in her chair, numb and speechless. She looked over again to the orchids. There they were, as always, a sanctuary, a purity.

She felt, above all, the seriousness of her responsibility to this new information. An office romance—love, adoration, puppy love, lust? Half-recognized, not fully appreciated, it seems—spurned? by the *secretary*? A nice young lawyer, bright future with the firm, in a dalliance, or worse. He was likely to fritter it all away in unprofessional chats and whispers, confidences betrayed in warm embraces. What did young people *do* these days? Did they date? She doubted they had that much class. From what Nancy could tell, they just trundled into cohabitation, so long as the peg fit into the hole. She and her husband, in any case, had had the decency to date and date for a long time—before taking that step toward the physical. By the time they did make the move, they had fairly determined its consequences. It wasn't a surprise anymore; it had become a function, an outcome, part of the package.

But none of this had a place here at Grecko Mauster Crill.

•

"Ladies and gentlemen," Bill said, swinging back in a conference chair. "We're pleased to have had a certain change in fortune here at the firm. With the advent of Palm Consulting, as well as the addition of the lovely and formidable Sandy Spires, it now seems we are once again working in the black. I, for one, am grateful to Sandy for her work with Palm, but also for consulting with me about various other matters. The woman has her hands in everything! Anyway, I want you all to be warned: we are going to be very busy around here. And to kick off this season of prosperity . . . Sandy? Are you prepared to speak to this august assembly?"

"Thank you, Bill. In the past couple of weeks, you have all been a great help to me in getting settled here at Grecko Mauster Crill. I appreciate it. Rex has been working like a dog, and Winona—Winona gets me everything I need. Everyone's been on board. At this point, we need to start looking toward the future. Bill and Umar have asked me to help them with long-range thinking about the firm's priorities. I am more than pleased to do so, and I will be asking you all for assistance as I assess our policies and workloads. Bill and Umar—and Mr. Grecko, too, rest his soul—have made a thriving, sturdy house here; now we're aiming to make it a castle. But the first step is simply letting you all know how much we appreciate you here, and locking in your slavish good work for the future."

Bill started pulling out of his breast pocket a stash of what looked like envelopes. Then he thrust them back in, provoking a nervous/gleeful titter in the room.

"C'mon, Bill. Hand them over," said Umar.

"Yes, yes. Here you go," he said. He then passed out envelopes to Rex, Nancy, Winona, and Lucy. "A little token of our appreciation."

"It's springtime!" Umar cried. "Go buy a rabbit or a chick or a motorcycle. Go take your loved ones out to dinner."

Back at her desk, Winona slid a new document under the blue ruler. *Dear Mr. Brand: We are in receipt of your letter* . . .

Things had certainly taken a turn; what a lucky afternoon! She had never gotten a bonus before. At the end of the Sunday-night shift at Elinor's restaurant, Elinor had distributed the baked goods that had gone unsold during the weekend, and jars of leftover soup. It was a boon, certainly, but not really a bonus. A thousand dollars! In one shot. She felt, just then, indispensable. She really *did* fit in; she really *was* working toward something with all the good people on the fifty-eighth floor.

3 ↝

Who can deny the force of beauty? Winona was lulled into admiration by the outfits the blind woman wore, and how sexy she was, how scary/gorgeous with those blue-gray oval glasses like halogen lamps or equipment from a science lab. To Winona, Sandy seemed of-a-piece, extra-terrestrial, while she herself felt like the compilation of many things, and decidedly regular.

Still, with Sandy it was always type this, type that, just like with everyone else. Instead of Bill and Umar's favored yellow pads, Sandy handed Winona disks with documents in need of formatting, or she used tapes. Winona had dusted off the Dictaphone and reacquainted herself with the foot pedal. She could make Sandy's voice fast and high as a chipmunk on acid, or she could slow it down until she sounded deeply retarded. Either way, the letters were succinct and smart and rivaled Bill in chill and accomplishment.

Sandy was, more than anything, a professional, a no-nonsense kind of go-getter. So it was a surprise when, that Wednesday evening, after they'd worked until seven and were just waiting around for the messenger, she placed herself in the Mr. Ed window and started to chat. She smoothed the lapel of her just-so jacket.

"Elizabeth Arden is having a two-for-one special on their Day of Beauty. Want to come with me on Saturday, my treat? Would do us both good to get out of here."

Winona had never been invited to a Day of Beauty by a beautiful, blind lawyer before. But Saturday was also the couples' conference.

Day of Beauty: leisure, luxury, elegance? Astonishing potential for female partnership, a chance for prolonged company with someone who wore clothes purchased by a personal shopper? Couples' conference: the moment of truth with Jeremy? To break up before or after? The fearsome recollection that Jeremy had, just last night, confided that he was now feeling that much closer to "going the distance," i.e., succumbing to his animal instinct after all, i.e., making love to her? Until now, she had avoided the inevitable conversation. But now this, a sign of some kind.

"Okay," she said, feeling a rush, the acceleration of life around her.

•

To Rex, love was serious business. He had more or less hit bottom the month before—on Valentine's Day, to be specific. It wasn't that anything horrible had happened; no one threw roses back in his face; stood him up for dinner; posed herself, kissing another, at his front door. No, it wasn't any of those things, though such scenarios had cinematic appeal. What happened to him could be summed up by his selection of groceries compared to those of the guy in front of him at the store. The other guy's groceries: a bottle of champagne, a faithless little branch of purple flowers, a heart-shaped box of chocolates with a big red bow. Rex's groceries: bathroom cleanser, a loaf of white bread, a bottle of Sprite, a half-pound of roast beef, a bag of barbecue flavored potato chips. It wasn't so much the alone-before-*The Simpsons* aspect of his meal that bothered him, but rather, alas, the everyday, take-no-risks quality of it.

Food is food, what does it matter, he told himself glumly on his walk up Madison, past a man selling paintings of New York and another with piles of sticky, hot peanuts. He hadn't taken a risk in years. He might never take a risk again. Law school wasn't a risk. It was hard work, but not a risk. There was the general risk of living, but that didn't seem to count. He couldn't call himself a daredevil just because he was an animate object on the planet. Winona took risks. There was something peculiarly risky about her. Love was the riskiest thing in the world, Rex thought, looking up at the bruised sky, still luminous between the silver and black boxes of buildings. Love was the riskiest, but he, until now, had been one of the quiet cowards of the sidewalk, swilling soda, watching TV, waiting for the adventure.

Of course, he had drunk beer with the others in col-

lege, and he had done one or two memorably dumb
things at two or three in the morning. And also, Rex
reminded himself, no one could deny that you actually
did need to make a way for yourself in the world, mater-
ially speaking. You had to take control of your life.
Although when he told himself this, waiting on the corner
for the light to change, listening to snippets of Protestant
bickering from the woman in the fur coat and the gray-
haired man at her side, he also reluctantly acknowledged
that the pressure to go to law school didn't exactly come
from him. There was his fierce tribe of blood relatives,
too, of course. Still, he couldn't be faulted for *this,* his career, if he could just break out elsewhere.

So on the cold Valentine's Day street corner, he'd had
a minor revelation. He would be a little more courageous
when it came to women. He didn't exactly mean
"women"; he meant Winona.

Winona. Surely she was Irish, with her sweet exuber-
ance, that constant milkmaid optimism, the golden glow
of the misinformed. And she was so tall. Not too tall—not
a geek or a stork—but long and gently curving, like a
stretch of ribbon. He wondered if her hair was naturally
striped. *His* hair was all one shade—wasn't most people's?
Hers was blond, brown, bronze—and he wanted to touch
it, to flip over that little flop that was always getting in her
eyes. He wanted to touch the hollow between her thin
shoulders and her melon-cup breasts, the prairie terrain
of her heart.

But in the wake of their date, so longed for, things
didn't look entirely hopeful. This morning they'd run into
each other in the basement store.

"Oh, hi, Rex," she'd said, like he'd just asked her for a quarter. "What's up?"

"Just picking up some snacks for later," he said, grabbing a bag of chips off the rack.

They walked through the Chrysler Building's basement hall, over black and gray and white marble squares. They just missed one elevator, full of office workers, and the next one that came was theirs alone. He tried not to look at her.

"So, did you ever get my message? I called you over the weekend."

"Oh, yes, I did, but, thanks, I—"

"I had a good time, you know."

"Me, too," Winona said, glancing up at him.

Then he said: "Friends, right?"

"Yeah. Is that okay?"

"I love it," Rex said. The door opened to their floor. "I need friends. Friends are what I live for."

So there they were. And now Rex was back at his desk, the specter of Bill looming over him as surely as Anthony Grecko hung over Lucy in the front hall.

Bill Mauster—Rex tried to tell himself that he was like a coach, or maybe a teacher, but he couldn't fix on any goodwill or charity behind the brusque exterior. It was all brusque exterior. Still, Rex found him brilliant as an attorney, and it almost seemed that appreciating brilliance was one part of the equation, and that the Brilliant One would also feel his appreciation and they'd thrive together in a symbiotic relationship.

Rex hunkered down before an agreement at his desk,

using his toolbox of laws and logic. He felt fairly certain he could make it a little bit better. But perfect, brilliant? There was always the missing link to worry about, the absence Mauster would point out later.

Was this what it meant to be a lawyer?

4

The room was heady with the scent of eucalyptus, lavender, citrus, rosemary. A row of tiny recessed lights circled the room like a diamond tiara. Winona and Sandy wore fluffy white towels and sat, facing forward, in twin, light-blue, Naugahyde recliners.

"So you were an English major, huh?" Winona asked.

"Yes, well, at first I was a psychology major, but it wasn't at all interesting to me. Then I went for English—the great Romantics. But what was I going to do as a blind English major? Become a braille librarian? Write a little redemption memoir? I don't think so. But law is egalitarian. It's like a game. You just need to know the rules."

"I thought of becoming a lawyer myself, once. That was after I read *Bartleby the Scrivener*." There was something about the setting, Winona thought, that made it easy to confide in each other.

"Bartleby—a first-class loser."

"A loser? No way—he's a force of nature."

Sandy laughed and adjusted her glasses. "That's funny, Winona. You must have very low standards of excellence."

"I don't—I just appreciate the mundane, the triumph of the ordinary against the great kings."

"Appreciating the mundane? I'd rather be the king any day."

"Well, let's put it this way," Winona said. "There are just certain qualities that old Bartleby has, I don't know. They make me feel vindicated. I wouldn't mind being a king—okay, a queen—but I don't want subjects, see what I mean?"

"You're talking about power, the responsibilities therein. You need to choose one or the other, Winona. It's as simple as that. For every winner there's a loser. Choose your battlefield."

"I prefer not to."

"Very funny."

They sat in silence for a moment.

"Bartleby. What a loser," Sandy said.

"Bartleby is timeless, like Santa Claus."

"You know who's timeless? Marcus Aurelius. Machiavelli. Napoleon."

"That's a whole different ball game. That's old school."

"Old school? It's the only school."

"There's a different kind of power in the world than brute strength."

"Yes, there's brute strength combined with intelligence."

"Or there's the power of art. Is your face beginning to shrink?" The last (and only) facial Winona had had was when she was a teenager and her friend had given her a sticky pink Mary Kay makeover.

"Yeah, it's this clay. It wants your blood."

"Anyway, the power of art and all that."

"Ha!" Sandy said. "You're funny."

Winona didn't know what to say. All her life people had been telling her that. Not so much, *You really should try out for* Saturday Night Live; more like, *What the fuck are you talking about?*

In a little while Sandy said: "Go on, you can ask me."

"Ask what?"

"Ask the blind questions."

"Blind questions? What blind questions?"

"I could see when I was a kid, and then it started dimming. The whole world dimmed around me. They made me wear these patches, but then when they took them off, I couldn't see anything. That was the beginning."

"Really? How old were you?"

"I was seven," Sandy said, then she was quiet.

Winona breathed in and out the strong brew of herbal intoxicants. The air around them was getting thicker.

Sandy's voice resumed. "For months, I just wanted to stay in the little corner of the world that I had seen, so I could imagine it. New shapes and sounds and smells clobbered me, they came so fast."

"It sounds scary."

"Did you think it would be like going to sleep and dreaming?"

"It's just that you seem so composed."

"Everything changes, that's inevitable. Try closing your own eyes for a minute. The world has a new order. What is it?"

"Oh, sorry. I was just thinking about this guy I know. At night when the lights are off it seems like he's shouting in my ear, but it's just his natural speaking voice, amplified, I guess, by the dark."

"Everyone shouts at me. They get their compassionate responses confused. Half the time they think I'm dumb. Is this shouting man your boyfriend?"

Winona's face prickled under the Mediterranean clay, and she said no.

"Just someone you picked up and sleep with, then?"

"We were together, but it didn't really work out."

They had met for coffee. Jeremy seemed to sense what was going on even before she said anything. Still, Winona had gone through with the painful, overused words soon after they placed their orders. When the waitress returned, they were just staring in separate directions like statues on either side of a driveway. The waitress placed the cups in front of them and went to another table. Jeremy threw his paper napkin down (not as dramatic as cloth) and swore. Then he was gone. She drank her café au lait carefully, leaving his to cool in the air.

"Happens most of the time," said Sandy.

"What about you?"

She shrugged. "It's not really my thing."

"Thing? I thought love was for everyone."

The door opened and let in a wedge of jarring light. Two women in white coats descended on them and peeled off their masks. One of the beauty consultants took Winona's elbow and led her out of the room.

It was time for an *Organic Submersion,* which had something to do with toxins and the replenishment of the spirit's floral-partner essences, and then a massage.

•

Winona had had massages before, sure, but not frequently and not, in any real sense, satisfactorily. Massages, as it turned out, were expensive. In college, certain hippie friends gave them to each other, but Winona worried about hippies. She worried about patchouli, clove, and garlic most of all. She worried about underarm hair—her own, yes, but mostly that of others. With hippie-girl massages, there was the expectation that you would turn over and return the favor, which was all right under certain, but not all, circumstances. There had been—in high school and also in college—the prelude to and/or stand-in-for sex massage. It was the kind Jeremy might give in a move toward intimacy. But the prelude massage, to Winona's thinking, was a fake: a person could not relax if the entire plot was to get her to relax. "Relaxing" didn't come easy like that. "Relaxing" didn't come at the hands of an odd male person who at any moment might desist in his methodical caress and drop his hand down like an inquiring fox.

So that only left the paid-for massage, which was the best kind, but depressing in its own way, paying for physical touch and all that. Winona remembered one time—

perhaps it was the last time—lying on a special massage table with her head facing downward in a spot cut out for that purpose. She'd gazed at the peach-colored rug as the masseuse turned down the lights. When she'd touched Winona, Winona had begun to cry; she didn't know why. An on switch had been flipped. She'd watched her tears plink silently down on the carpet.

Now the new woman placed her hands on Winona's skin. Winona closed her eyes. She thought about Jeremy, alone, maybe at the conference, taking solitary notes. They could have been holding hands, fingers splayed, libidos closed, ready to build a relationship like a brick wall.

But Jeremy, he had been a friend, anyway, and now they weren't even that anymore.

●

"So, Winona, you told me the other day that you hadn't really planned on being a secretary. Does that mean you'll be leaving us soon for bigger and better things?"

They were back in the lavender room, "letting their muscles settle," according to their guides.

"Oh, no. I like Grecko Mauster Crill. It's great, really. Especially—especially since you came."

"So what's your motivation for working?"

"My motivation?"

"Yes."

"Well, you know, the ethic of hard work, that type of thing."

"Right. What else?"

"Unfortunately, I've got some debt, a little debt, and I've got to dig myself out of that or I don't know what will happen. Ultimately I'd like to save money for a project I'm planning."

"What kind of project?"

"I've got an MFA in film, and, well, I want to make one."

"I see."

"But it's pretty much an inside-of-my-head deal at this point."

"A pipe dream?"

"I'm working on the screenplay. That bonus I got means I can buy a video camera and start experimenting with scenes."

"I thought you were going to pay off your debt."

"Well, yeah, but a bonus—a cheerful, goodwill bonus—"

"What's the film going to be about?"

"Um, a woman."

"This is what we'd call a soft sell."

"Okay, it's a point-of-view type of thing, about this woman and how she lives her life, and how strange it all seems."

"Uh-huh."

"She's a sexy woman, with a mysterious past."

"Good, good."

"And she's having a *very* strange day."

"It's *very* strange."

"It's so strange, that it's like, it's like science fiction, only it's just her everyday life, see what I mean?"

"Not really."

"I'm trying to capture the ineffable anxiety of living, you know? The Strange and/or Sexy Woman Meets Ineffable Anxiety."

"I've got a friend who produces films. I should introduce you to him."

"What kind of films?"

"I don't know. Sylvester's one of those young movers and shakers, from what I can gather, very well off at this point. A couple of years ago, we won his company quite a lot of money."

"The more contacts I have in the industry—"

The wedge of light returned. "All right, ladies, back to the real world," said a woman in white.

Winona and Sandy were ushered into separate dressing rooms. Winona's clothes seemed threadbare and unlaundered compared to her body, now as pampered as Cleopatra's. If only she had the type of outfit worn by an up-and-coming filmmaker, currently working closely with an independent production studio headed by a mover and shaker. No. No way. Sylvester: it sounded like some tartanwearing mouse from Hibernia.

When Winona came out to meet her in the front room, Sandy was sitting on a brocade couch by the fireplace.

"Sandy, I have to tell you, this has been so great. Thank you."

"Yes, it *was* fun, wasn't it?" Sandy said, with what seemed briefly like regret.

•

Monday morning Winona arrived early, wearing a purple jacket with black trim and a matching skirt. She'd gotten her hair cut over the weekend—just a trim—completing the beauty makeover. Her regular stylist, Jax, hadn't been available, so she'd had her hair done by Dot—a postmodern Dot, not the old Clip 'n' Curl girl. (This one looked like Louise Brooks with gardening shears. Surly, gloomy, silent—she made Winona feel guilty for being so utterly, unbearably unfashionable, and actually for just being there at all.)

Spending time with Sandy had made Winona's molecules tumble, her compass go haywire. How fascinating she was, and they'd had such a good time together! The law profession was populated with interesting and unique people, links to film, links to beauty. Maybe it wasn't so bad after all.

It wasn't a Lisa Box, but there was a new optimism in the air.

Winona tossed off a greeting to Anthony Grecko, then walked into the storage room to start a pot of coffee. While she was in there she picked up the faxes: one from a travel agency, one from the city clerk's office, and one from Brenda Blitzen. Brenda's was sent from her lawyer's office, a short note requesting an extension on the house inventory.

Winona knew that Brenda's stationery was pink, in original, and that the *B*'s of *Brenda* and *Blitzen* were gold embossed. The gold didn't come through on the fax, however, so it looked like the letter was from *renda litzen*. It was sad. Winona had never met Brenda, but she always imagined her as being on the breakable side, a carefully assembled china doll. Word around the office was that Ron had put Brenda through a half-dozen surgeries before he'd proposed to her.

Good morning, Nancy; good morning, Rex. Winona dropped off her purse and turned on the computer. She slipped new issues of *Harper's* and *Smithsonian* under a folder.

Bill's door was closed. She listened, heard nothing, knocked.

Nothing still. She knocked again, this time with words attached. "Good morning, Mr. Mauster?"

She heard a noise from within and cracked open the door. "Coffee?"

Bill looked up. His glasses teetered midway down his nose.

"A little caffeine to start the day?" Smile.

"Oh, Winona. Yes, yes, coffee."

"Great! I'll be right back with it, and here's a couple of faxes."

Winona left and came back, averting her eyes from Bill's as she sought a patch of green on the paper-strewn blotter. She set down the cup, clasped her hands together in an attitude of mild supplication, then pivoted like a ballerina.

"Winona," Bill said, "I've got some things here. Just give me a minute."

"Certainly."

She sat down and Bill handed her back the Brenda Blitzen fax. "Copy this for Umar, our resident lonely-hearts specialist." Then he started handing her pink telephone message slips, one after another.

"Call him back and tell him I'll call later this afternoon. Call her and find out what she wants—I could call her back later in the week. Set up a time that will work for her on Friday, let's see, between eleven and one."

The last two slips were both from Doug Sandwitz, the Stratosphere lawyer.

"This prick thinks he can sell me a hamburger if he

calls it ground beef. He thinks he can sell me a hamburger if he calls it Le Hamburger. El Hamburgero. I'm sick of talking to him. Have Umar call him back."

"Umar's out today."

"That's right. Have Sandy call him. Sic *her* on Dougie boy. That should keep him quiet for a while."

Bill Mauster sat again, took off his glasses, and swiveled for a look out the window. It was a nice day; blue had seeped into the windows of the building across the way. Winona looked, too, to see what he saw.

"She's good," he said, as if to himself. "She's a carnivore."

Winona opened her mouth to say something, but then closed it again. Bill swung forward. "Take a letter to John Lazur. *Dear Johnny . . .*"

Winona grabbed a pen from Bill's desk and scribbled on the office supply brochure, sentences intertwined now with photos of pencil holders and tape dispensers.

•

"Hey Sandy, how's it going?" Winona said, looking at the recumbent white stick resting on the wall, then the deerlike legs Sandy held to one side of her chair. Sandy was extracting knowledge in some mysterious way from her computer.

"Just fine, Winona."

"The Day of Beauty set the tone for my whole weekend. I even got my hair cut on Sunday," Winona said.

Sandy slowed down in what she was doing. "I'm sorry to say I came in to the office and worked with Bill on Sunday, but other than that, I agree with you. Listen, I'm going to have a whole set of documents to go out for Palm.

I'll have the tape for you in about twenty minutes and will need them typed and formatted ASAP."

"Absolutely."

"The other thing is this—can you close the door for a moment?"

"Of course," Winona said and shut the door.

"I feel fairly certain that Umar isn't handling the Lisa Box/Stratosphere matter as well as he could be, but I don't want to offend him or Bill. You can understand that, can't you? It would help if I could assess the situation privately and steer them from the backseat, as it were. Would you mind photocopying the documents in the financial and correspondence files for me, so I can scan them and have a look? This way, I can check things out discreetly, do what I need to do, with no hurt feelings."

"Sure, I can do that."

"Good."

"Anything else?"

"That's it for now. The Blane documents are my priority, and this other matter you can get to by the end of the day."

As Winona walked away, Sandy added: "I did enjoy the Day of Beauty, Winona."

"Me, too," Winona said, heady with friendship and responsibility.

Umar was still in court that afternoon, defending some hapless criminal. (He said he took the pro bono cases because he got a kick out of courtroom drama, but most everyone believed it was because he felt kind of sorry for those poor little criminal guys.) It was as good a time as any to get the file. Winona collected the Lisa Box pages strewn among Umar's nudie magazines and real-estate documents, stashed them in a big brown expandable envelope, and took the file to the storage room. She methodically copied pages. It took a half-hour, but no one else came in to use the photocopier or eat pretzels or get a fax the whole time she was in there.

5 ↙

Should artists like Days of Beauty? Should artists covet silk pantsuits from places like Bonwit Teller? Winona wondered, trailing her hand along the sleeves of the slate-gray jackets, jackets Sandy would wear. How was it that a blind woman dressed better than she did? When Winona deposited the thousand-dollar check in her bank account, she had made a mistake on the deposit slip and had to start over; she wasn't used to this many zeroes. (There had been her student loan checks, but that hadn't quite counted. She was still paying them off, and would be until she was older than Bill Mauster.) She had decided that she liked Beauty to the 30-percent mark: she was spending $700 on the camera and $300 on clothes. She should be sending it all to Chase Manhattan, but never mind that:

Big black boots.

Green boots.

Shiny stilettos.

Intricately laced camisoles in colors with no known name.

Camisoles that you reveal, slightly.

Underpants as works of art.

A "smoking" jacket.

A "traveling" jacket.

Pants with newly configured relationships to the hip and ankle; quite in.

Additional pants in alternate colors.

Blouses in different shading groups: smoky & muted; tenderly & exquisitely feminine; boldy & richly bright.

Scarves.

Belts.

Socks.

A variety of gloves, some childish, some sophisticated.

Perfumes to go with outfits.

Purses and briefcases.

The store itself smelled like riches. Three hundred dollars doesn't buy what it used to, she lamented.

•

"C'mon, Winona, we're going to lunch," Sandy said, slipping on a black leather jacket.

"What?"

"Let's go. I'm meeting Sylvester in SoHo; I thought you'd want to come along."

"Oh, well—okay. I was supposed to finish up the Bon-

Pizza filings with Rex today, but we could probably do it later—"

"Hurry up. I'll meet you by the elevators."

Winona saved the document she was working on and got her purse. She stopped in front of Rex's office. He was looking at her with a woebegone expression.

"Who's Sylvester?"

"Sylvester? Oh, he's just a film guy, I guess, someone Sandy knows." Winona tried to sound calm. He had a weird name, but he was still a film producer.

"Great, great. Throw me over for some cheap date with Mr. Slick and the femme fatale of the law profession."

"I'm not, I would never throw you over."

"Fine. I love collating. I got my JD for this."

"This could be good for my career. The guy's in film."

"Whatever. Well, *Babylon Five* is on tonight. It's in reruns, but who cares, I'll be crying anyway so I won't be able to follow it."

"Can't we do it this afternoon? Sandy's waiting for me at the elevator."

"Always Sandy," Rex said. "It's all about Sandy now."

Winona swung her new gray silk scarf around her neck in dramatic fashion.

"Hollywood awaits," she said, and left.

•

Thank God she wasn't paying for lunch.

The appetizers were, like, ten bucks.

They had a big green bottle of mineral water that the waiter poured into their wine glasses. Winona had been on the verge of ordering a Diet Coke when Sandy had ordered this for the table. Realizing her mistake, she watched Sandy from there on in. The waiter was prepared to give Sandy anything she wanted; it wasn't just that she couldn't read the menu—the menu was discarded.

But then there was Sylvester. Sylvester the Artist. The Film Producer. The marriage of Art and Commerce. The tall man. Tall, about forty, wearing a jacket over a T-shirt. Tall, forty, jacketed, blue-eyed. Tall, forty, jacketed, blue-eyed, built. Tall, forty, jacketed, blue-eyed, built, charming. Didn't talk much. Used his eyes to describe things, things like attraction. Drank the Pellegrino water. Ordered, also, a scotch. Neat.

Hands. Hands big on the small glass of neat scotch.

"It was a simple case of deception," Sandy was saying. "The client had no idea that his wife could do that. He cherished his marriage—that's what he had told me, unbidden, I might add—and they had the house, the dog, the two kids, the church. Who would even think she'd rip the fabric of this wholesome thing they shared? And that is the beauty and the terror of it, the overwhelming vastness of ignorance."

"You continue to astonish me," Sylvester said.

"You say that to all the women."

"With you, it's true."

Yet when he said that he looked at Winona. Winona felt that her new gray scarf, her bob, perhaps even something further within, was having an encounter.

Sandy said: "And then there's Winona. At the office, everything is in her capable hands."

"I'm certain that's true."

"But she's got her eye on bigger things. That's why I wanted you to meet."

Winona clutched her vast white linen napkin. This was her cue.

"What Sandy means is that I'm working on—or at least would like to be working on—a film project."

"Oh? What's it about?" asked Sylvester.

"Sorry, as her attorney I advise that she not try to answer that."

"No, Sandy, I've got a new plug: it's about a woman who sees things."

"Ahh . . ."

"We're working on Winona's presentation."

"Sexy woman. Things of significance."

"Let's start with a title. Does it have a title?"

"*The Anxiety of Everyday Objects,*" Winona said.

"Sounds interesting," Sylvester said, but then his cell phone rang.

When he stepped back to the table, their entrées had arrived, and they were on to new topics.

The food was good, involving many different plates and sauces that Winona never actually got a handle on. She discreetly dipped everything everywhere.

After espresso, Sylvester took out a pen from within his jacket, turned over the bill and wrote: *Will you have a drink with me later tonight?* It was, you'd have to agree, a romantic moment.

•

Winona closed her eyes for a few seconds, trying to see if she could tell something essential about the day just by feeling the wind around their bench or the scent of the passersby and the trees and the hot dog vendor. She opened them again.

She took a drag of the cigarette Sandy had given her. The two women sat together on the bench, legs crossed, cigarettes held close to their chins, one white cane resting between them.

People kept looking at Sandy.

"I did have a girlfriend, actually, in law school," she was saying.

"Really?" Winona said, trying not to sound too interested or alarmed.

"We were in the same class, Ethics. At first she'd just stand close. I could feel her there. Then finally she talked to me. We argued about ethics—how prosaic is that? But the argument was just kindling."

People were hurrying past, flights from wives and husbands and jobs and histories. Winona closed her eyes a second time. The air was white, then chaotic. You couldn't tell if people were coming at you or not.

"Then what happened?" Winona asked, taking a drag of her cigarette.

"It was a total failure, finally, but for a minute or two, a few months—" Sandy paused. They were on the deck of an ocean liner, staring out at an endless sea. "There was an elegance to her, a purity. It made me believe in her for a time. And then, of course, there was her scent. That woman smelled like, I don't know, the Queen of the Nile. Surrender was the only possibility."

Winona placed one hand over the other, her fingers chapped and stiff with the falseness of spring.

"Jesus, I could hardly get any work done—that smell on my fingers, the recollection of her body placed behind mine, insinuating."

"Bad for business," Winona found herself saying. You had to say something.

"Then something happened to her. She started talking about leaving her girlfriend, moving in together."

"So she had a girlfriend?"

"Cling, cling, cling. People have to understand not to *lean*. To lean is dangerous, don't you think?"

"Well, they say that true intimacy, blah blah blah."

"Exactly. And to my way of thinking, so-called intimacy doesn't come unless you are truly yourself. Unless you walk on your own, embrace your possibility."

"Yes, then if you *do* finally meet someone nice, the two of you can stand next to each other. Like telephone poles or something," Winona said uncertainly. (What did *intimacy* really mean? She couldn't buy it at a store or a conference, she felt sure of that. Did it just sweep people up? Was there a thrill to it?)

In the cab on the way back Sandy said: "You know, I've taken a look at those Lisa Box files and, I don't know, it doesn't seem like they're complete. Are you sure you gave me everything?"

"Everything we have, yes. But you know Umar—sometimes he files things in his head between Ditz and Fluff. I think half the time he keeps things to himself, not because he's secretive, but just because he forgets other people are interested."

"We'll have to work on him. A man like that—"

"A fish without a bicycle, right?" Winona said. "Look at that. The dogwoods are blossoming."

•

Perhaps it's time to review Winona's romantic history. Where to begin, where, really, to end? It sounds pompous to say: she had loved. Nor would the *count* do—crass, too crass, not that we aren't frank here. Or the whos; we have the list of whos. Love accommodates to whatever shape is required: sweaty men with manners, men who drink tea and men who run marathons, men in tweed jackets with thunderous voices, men who do not, in fact, make a sound. When it comes down to it, love seems to fit, somehow, one and all. She had not known, it could be said, a *defining* relationship. The repeating characteristic had been a certain distance. Whether that distance came from an unbalanced madness—she loved, he didn't; he loved, she didn't—or a peculiarity of geography, or duration, or even a dimness of feeling all around, it all seemed to come down to the same thing: Winona remained unchanged. She was steady and happy thus, and, though she wept like all spurned lovers, the trajectory of her life remained the same. (You wouldn't call Jeremy the Sincere a spark to gunpowder.)

And yet, here she was. A dark bar, a corner. A man with glittering eyes and a shared love for film, with his hand provocatively close to her leg. Waiting there. As if time had stopped. As if this were some sort of poem. As if this Poire Williams, or whatever he had called it, wasn't just another splash of booze but the elixir of Desire.

"I don't even go to the movies anymore. I find so many of them a trifle boring," Sylvester was saying.

"Really?" Winona said. "I guess I always get swept up in them, even if they are dumb."

"Do you really waste all that time in the dark?"

"I can see in the dark," she said, though she felt rather silly about it afterward.

He smiled. "Can I get us a couple more drinks?"

She watched Sylvester go up to the bar. He was very tall, and better dressed than the fools and charlatans that surrounded them. Before this, he had been telling her about the time he spent in France working on scripts with some important personages from Paris, Mexico City, and Toronto. He was buying the drinks; there was no question of her paying. She was still wearing her new gray scarf.

"So, Winona—beautiful name for a beauty—tell me a little more about your screenplay," he murmured, placing a fresh glass before her.

"Well, you know how, let's say, you're driving down a road and you see a store, and you think it says TEMPORARY FASHIONS, but then you keep driving and a tree or a corner peels away and you realize it says CONTEMPORARY FASHIONS? How there's something about the first illusion that reveals something new and real about the world? Or if you pass a church, say, and the letters on the marquee are supposed to spell FIND YOUR PERSONAL LORD but the *rd* is missing so it says FIND YOUR PERSONAL LO, like *loo*, y'know, the British word for bathroom?"

"I know the word."

"Okay, so the film is about that."

"About what?"

"About seeing. About a woman who can actually see all this stuff, see what I mean? So things that were kind of ordinary are totally not ordinary anymore. In a way, it's very Zen. It's very, very Zen."

Winona took another sip of the pear liqueur. "Just today I realized that it could actually be, in a weird kind of way, about blindness."

"So this is where Sandy comes in?"

"Yes, but don't mention it—I don't want to tell her yet. It might make her feel self-conscious."

"I don't tell her anything," he said conspiratorially.

"I wish I could find out what she's really thinking, you know?"

"That'll never happen. Eventually you just end up accepting Sandy, warts and all."

"Warts? She has warts?"

"Not warts, but—proclivities, say. Sandy's main concern is always herself."

"But she helped you a lot, right?"

"Sure, we made more money through that case than we've ever made through actual films. In a way, she's a very creative person."

The jewel-like shimmer of the alcohol diminished and diminished until it was only a tiny gleaming ray at the bottom of the glass, and Sylvester and Winona were both slumped on the bench, looking out at the other patrons.

"These people, they don't even go to films," he lamented.

"But neither do you, you said so yourself."

"Ah, but it's different."

"Really?"

"I'm like the weary walrus, who has seen too much of

122

the world. These guys . . . these guys are like the weary—
the weary—I don't know . . ."

"Weevils? Weary weevils?

"Yes, the hoards of weevils. Even film buffs—they call
themselves *buffs*, mind you—would rather argue about
Grace Kelly versus Tippi Hedren than experience something new, simple, beautiful. Art is about seeing something for the first time, you understand, not rewinding a
tape on your VCR to verify, for the tenth time, the couch
color in *Rear Window*."

"I see what you're saying. Yes, I like that. Seeing
something for the first time."

"The films we produce—mostly underground projects from Berlin, some from New Jersey—are impas-
sioned, articulate, deviant. But most of all, they're just art.
Art. It's as simple as bread and wine. That's really all I
want in life."

Winona stared at the curve of his delicate collar, a cut
recently introduced by the fashion industry to confuse
the regular citizen.

"That's really all?"

"No, not all," he said, turning toward her, touching,
for a millisecond, the hair by her temple. "Not everything, but almost."

6 ⌇

When Winona got to the office the next day Rex was doing sprints for Bill. "REEEEEEX!" roared Bill, like an official calling out laps at the track. "Morning!" Rex said to Winona as he flew down the hall, holding his tie in one hand, a document in the other. "Morning," she said back, and they rolled their eyes at each other. Now that Winona had arrived, they both knew, Bill would transfer some orders to her.

And he did, but between tasks Winona typed and wondered if, perhaps, she would get a call from Sylvester—the kind gentlemen make, the next-day murmur. As usual, Lucy took most of the calls at the office, but when it rang twice, Winona picked up.

"Good afternoon? Grecko Mauster Crill?" she said,

modulating her tone midway from Cheerful Secretary to
Suave Artist.

"Winona? Is that you?"

Liz sounded irritated, as if she hadn't just made the
call, but rather had been interrupted ten minutes before
the end of her weekly mystery show. She could probably
tell, with sisterly hocus-pocus, that Winona was once
again distracted.

"Oh. Yes."

"How are you doing?"

"I'm fine, how are you?" Winona said, falling into step.

"Oh fine, you know, busy. God! My job has been *insane*
lately! I mean, my boss, she's out of control. I don't know
what to say about her. We're working hard all the time,
though, I tell you. Overtime galore—not that I take any of
it—and I haven't had a vacation in, God, years! And that's
why I'm calling. I've been invited to Chez Shimmy in the
Bahamas for four nights and I'm wondering—"

"Chez Shimmy? Sounds like a *very* low-rent
Club Med."

"It's not at all like Club Med, Winona. This is a cook-
ing school and resort. It's really called 'Chez Simone de
Poisson' but those in the know call it Chez Shimmy. Anyway, little Sniffles will be *soooo* lonely while I'm gone . . ."

"Just keep the screens in and he won't jump out the
window."

"Oh, Winona!"

"Isn't there a twelve-step program for dog loneliness?"

"You're so funny I forgot to laugh," Liz said.

"Yeah, well."

Aurelie Sheehan

"Winona, can you take care of him? It's the last weekend in April."

Winona thought about Fruit Bat, her poor, beautiful, spider-plant-eating feline. Alone. In the dark. A sacrifice.

"Sure, Liz. I can do it. I just hope Fruit Bat will be okay."

"Oh, cats. They don't need any attention!"

"Yes they do!"

"C'mon, cats just need a barrel of food and a rubber mouse or something. Sniffles needs to be *walked*. And he gets *lonely*. He really does. Then he starts chewing stuff up."

"He's got your number, huh?"

Let's see, Winona thought, if Sniffles had *Liz's* number, and Liz had *Winona's* number, then, really, Winona was being bossed around by a schnauzer. Not that they aren't lovable.

"For Christ's sake, Winona, I'm just calling my own sister for a little bit of a favor. Why is everything such a fight with you?"

Winona mumbled something back, got the details, and even agreed to the oft-promised "drinks after work" Liz speculated about when these sorts of arrangements had been finalized. She got off the phone and returned to her in-box.

•

"*Yoo-hoo*," Nancy's voice rang out from down the hall the next morning. "Donuts!"

Winona remained still before her computer.

"Yoo-hoo!"

Winona got up. She looked in on Umar on her way down the hall. He had his feet up on his desk and was studying an important think piece on American culture in *Penthouse*, oblivious to any rearrangement of his papers.

"Yoo-hoo," Winona whispered into his room. He jumped, closing his magazine and tossing it, facedown, on the desk. It slid off onto the floor.

"What?" he said.

"Donuts."

"Donuts? Right. I'll be right there."

Rex joined Winona in the hall, and when they got to the front, Nancy was unwrapping the pink-and-orange paper from a box of Dunkin' Donuts. There they were. Boston cream. Cinnamon. Cruller.

"I thought it was a perfect day for a treat," said Nancy.

She was wearing a pink mandarin-collared suit with a lighter pink blouse underneath. She looked at Winona, and then at Rex, her eyes narrowing.

"Oh, wow," said Winona.

"Great idea," said Lucy, leaning over the counter. "May I?"

"Of course. Now, everybody, please, help yourself. I'm sure you already are."

"Say what?" said Rex.

"I just meant, if you haven't already had breakfast."

"This is so nice, Nancy," Winona said, reaching for a cruller.

"Can't resist!" said Rex.

"Crullers. That's very sophisticated, Winona. Aren't you the grown-up girl?"

"Thanks, Nancy," Winona said. She was having a two-star day, according to her horoscope.

Umar appeared, rubbing his palms together. "Oh, joy! I'm hungry, deeply hungry."

"Speaking of sophistication," Nancy continued. "I was thinking we might get plaques with our names on them for outside our office doors—or for our desks, of course," she added with an ingratiating smile.

"Rex Willard: Slouch and Hacker," Rex said.

"No, Rex. You're a lawyer, *remember*?" Nancy said.

"Rex Willard: Gone Fishing," he continued.

"Rex Willard: Man of Action," said Winona.

"What does that mean?" asked Nancy.

"Nothing," Winona said.

"He's an *attorney*."

"Chill, Nancy. Didn't you know that lawyers can be superheroes, too? We change clothes in phone booths, don't you know."

Rex leaped backward as a blob of jelly made its way out of his donut.

Bill and Sandy came in together from the front hall. He was holding her arm. For a moment, framed at the entrance, they looked like bride and groom, a kind of nightmare of heterosexual accomplishment. He was an old man, so comfortable in his gray suit, white shirt, and gold tie dotted with small fleurs-de-lis that it was hard to imagine him ever looking any differently—in a hot tub, for instance. Or washing a car. And then there was the bride: slim, young, beautiful. She stood still and cool as a statue (sniffing donuts?). *It's me. I'm the chosen one.* Chiseled face, full lips held carefully together.

"Donuts?" Bill said, like he'd never heard of them before.

Later, Bill was passing Winona in the hall and said, "Er . . .
Winona, can you please join me in my office?"

"Shall I get my pad?"

"Not necessary."

She followed him to his office and sat down in one of
the sleek leather chairs. Fruit Bat would like to get hold of
one of these. (How many adversaries has Bill skewered in
this chair? How many times has the recognition of defeat
taken hold of a person as they clutched the butter-soft
bolsters?)

Bill called Umar on the intercom, telling him to bring
Sandy.

Umar? Sandy? Winona was a little alarmed. Bill
punched in another number.

"Mr. Brinch."

Silence.

"Lou, it's me. Do you have a response to our memo of
March 20?"

Silence.

"We can't wait—fax it to me this morning."

Silence.

"Just do it, Lou." *Click.*

Umar ushered in Sandy, then stepped in himself and
closed the door. There was a general shuffling and murmur. Sandy sat in the chair next to Winona. Umar leaned
on the windowsill.

Bill took off his glasses and rubbed his eyes slowly,
pushing in with his splayed fingers, then pulling them
back to center. He squinted at Winona.

"Winona, have the March bills gone out yet?"

"Um—no. I usually wait until the last day of the month."

"I'd like you to turn that job over to Nancy."

"All right."

"Now, Miss Bartlett, a number of things have come up lately, thanks to Sandy's expertise and foresight. Various matters, but for our purposes right now, there's a sense that you, um, have a lot of potential, and—" Here Bill paused as if he'd lost his train of thought, then started up again. "Sandy and I have been talking, along with Umar, naturally, and we'd like to offer you a promotion, effective immediately. We'd like you to take over the role of office manager."

"Office manager?"

"Is there an echo in the room?" Bill said with a little smile. "Yes. Office manager. A promotion. Increased responsibility. And, of course, *ple-enty* more money."

He enunciated *plenty* like the *merry* of a Macy's Santa Claus.

"We feel you have some potential, Winona," Sandy added. "And we need to streamline operations around here. We need energy. We need commitment. You've got youth and common sense."

"Well," she said, rather brightly. "Thank you for thinking of me. But I guess my first question is, what about Nancy?"

"We'll take care of her," Bill said. "Nancy will actually retain many of her duties, but her title will more accurately reflect what she does here."

Sandy said, "Specifically, you'll take on more of a management position in terms of overseeing the rest of the staff and dealing with clients, and Nancy will work on background administration, such as bills and filing."

Umar looked out the window and chuckled. "The old gal may not like it much, Winona, but traditionally, the young do eat the old."

"Are you ready, willing, and able?" asked Bill.

"Yes, thank you. I'm flattered that you—I'm so glad that I can—"

"Your salary will go up five thousand dollars."

"I'll e-mail you the new job description this afternoon," Sandy said.

"Okay, great," said Winona, shifting to the edge of her chair, sensing the end of the conversation. "Thanks, guys."

•

Winona, career woman, went back to her typing.

> Furthermore, no remedy or promise was ever construed at the inception of the enterprise, nor was any implied in any way to the Shareholders. In plain language, what you assert in your letter makes no sense, rings no bell, in fact can be applied not at all to the present circumstance . . .

"You're not working, you're staring off into the middle distance!" Rex said, appearing in the Mr. Ed window.

"I *am* working, figuring out what just happened."

"What just happened?"

"I got a raise, and a promotion. I'm now the office manager."

"Oh, yeah, she goes into the Box and comes out an office manager! Next thing you know she'll be Steven Spielberg!"

"I don't want to be Steven Spielberg," growled Winona.

"*I* need to go in a Lisa Box—no, a Larry Box. I need to become a—a diplomat from a foreign country. Or a tenor with the Metropolitan Opera!"

Winona scrunched her face.

He continued: "No, no, really, that's great. Office manager. Cool. No one deserves it more than you. So anyway, what? You're going to start sending us memos on pink paper? Implement some new umbrella-storage policies?"

"That's the thing. What about Nancy? Bill called her in right after I left. Now she's in her office with the door closed."

"Nancy will survive, kiddo. Sandy probably has a plan for her, too."

"Sandy?"

"Sure, she's the engine of the new machine, man. Or the soul? Whatever. Umar is even talking about a retreat for the big boys—that includes me—in Scottsdale, Arizona, for a little golfing action! Look out world!"

"Calm down."

"I can't! Not in the presence of an *office manager.*"

"You are strange."

"No, no, no. You're the one with striped hair."

"Striped hair?"

"Streaked?"

"These are natural highlights. It said so right on the bottle."

"Ah! Well, Miss Herbal Essence, after all this, I still need you to get back to work. You're holding me up. I've got to get through with the Purdue lease before close of business."

"Yeah, yeah."

"Get to work, tiger."

•

That afternoon there was a little commotion in the hall. Winona heard Umar, his voice complicit and feverish.

"No, no, *listen*—it's not that he was *just* ineffectual in defending the client, he actually wanted this poor man to give him advice on his daughter's upcoming wedding. The client was in restaurants, and the little man complied, giving him—"

Winona swung her chair around and glimpsed Umar hovering over Sandy like a dromedary over a flower. He held her arm within his, guiding her toward his office, and tossed his gray curls as he relayed his mirthful tale.

"You might say it's another argument for maintaining a completely professional relationship with your clients," Winona heard Sandy say.

"Or does it mean that the client-attorney relationship is really just as debased as every other, and we might meditate on *them* when we're looking for clues to our own personal lives?"

"How debased are your personal relationships, Umar?"

"Oh, not debased enough by far."

"I'm sure."

Umar said: "On the other hand, client-attorney matters are just getting stickier—I think our old widower Garfield has a crush on me now. He was actually lying down on my couch when I came back to my office with the notarized copy of his will."

"Possibly he'd been dazzled to an early death by your supreme bullshit."

"Bullshit? Me? Oh, sweetheart—you break my heart in *two*."

"I don't think so. You don't even have a heart, do you?"

"Yes, feel it, here."

Winona *thinks* that's what he said at the end, but then Umar closed his door.

Winona went back to her document: *insert new paragraph here.*

7

"You are so lovely," Sylvester said from where he leaned, askew against the fake-leopardskin chair. He had called and asked if she wanted to go out: he knew a Russian restaurant that sold vodka in glasses shaped like snow geese.

His eyes were deeply deep and sexual and artistic, Winona thought. How interesting it all was, the core relationship between sex and art. Comparing his eyes to the 9–5 regimen at Grecko Mauster Crill was like comparing the dead to the living, nothing to everything important in the world!

"Thank you," she murmured, spinning her empty snow goose around and around.

"I couldn't stop thinking about you today."

"I thought of you, too," she admitted.

She felt a bit light-headed from the vodka; the caviar and toast bits hadn't done much to fill her stomach.

"I just found myself laughing sometimes, thinking about your movie."

"Really? Laughing?" She didn't know whether to be encouraged.

"You have a really—" He broke off with a chortle. "A really unique way of looking at things. In this world, it's so easy to get jaded, to lose track of what's important. I was sitting in this fucking meeting with these backers, you know, telling them what they want to hear about the German underground, etcetera, comparing it—I hate to admit this—to a sleek black Mercedes-Benz carrying contraband along the Autobahn, and I remembered your way of depicting your work. How pure it was."

"Well, pureness, uniqueness. That's great, but I, too, ultimately will need backers." She flushed when she said this, as if revealing something untoward.

"To hell with backers!" he said. "Let's get drunk and have our attorneys sue the bajangles off some rich assholes, and we'll back ourselves *that* way!"

"No, no. The strength of our ideas will pave the way to riches."

He started laughing again. "You are so pretty, but crazy, crazy. *Fou! Loco!* It's astonishing, really. Please, let's go back to my apartment. I can show you my etchings, I can reveal my feelings, whatever you want. Pretty please."

"Oh," Winona said. "It's a bit fast, isn't it?"

"But you can feel it, too, can't you? We can't pretend not to see what's happening."

His bedroom was virtually empty, not in college-student fashion, more in a monk/Pottery Barn sort of way. The bed, however, was strewn with a variety of cushions, odd shapes and textures, perhaps Turkish or Moroccan. They weren't entirely comfortable to lean against; they kept slipping.

They were sitting on the bed because the couch in the living room was covered by a tarp in preparation for the painting of the walls. They had glasses of red wine in their hands, and a box of Ritz crackers lay on the bed between them. ("Isn't it so kitsch?" he had said. "But I love them.") Sylvester had lit a candle and placed it on top of a stack of *ArtForum* magazines on the nightstand, next to the clock radio. Winona's eyes kept flipping from the flame (art, passion, love, the grand illusion) to the clock (weekday, Fruit Bat, hangover, birth control).

"I am tormented by them," he was saying. He was talking about his standards again.

Did he have condoms? Was she going to have sex tonight? This seemed like a novel idea. She could see the shape and insinuation of Sylvester's thighs under his pants. She looked at his big hands. They looked like a stranger's hands.

At some point, Sylvester picked up the box of crackers and placed them on the table. He was bigger than her, by far, and he was older and he was a film producer. His mouth tasted like wine; his Kenneth Cole shoes were now on the floor.

In the Chrysler Building lobby the next morning, Winona ran into Ron Blitzen. If this were *The Wizard of Oz*, he'd be the Tin Man before the business about the heart. Whenever she saw him, she always pictured him hunched over a bar stool at the strip club, before pinstripes and wingtips covered up the leer.

"Hello, Mr. Blitzen," she said, standing next to him by the elevator.

"Hello," he said, with a short nod. He seemed to know her just slightly, although they'd seen each other numerous times over the past year. It was frankly always worrisome to Winona when she encountered this man. Even before his separation from Brenda, she had felt as if he were looking at her like a specimen from Before, as in, from the Before/After pictures they have of women, mostly, on either side of treatments for acne, obesity, flat-chestedness, thin-lippedness, squints, pallors, bad attitudes, flaccid musculature, mousy hair, facial hair, bunions, hunchbacks, yellow teeth, crossed eyes, intellects, and proclivity toward punning. She imagined him meeting women, giving them a card for the nearest Lisa Box, with the suggestion that they get together only after she'd been Upgraded—done, changed, made better forever.

Of course, what woman would want to go out with such a scowler? But a scowling millionaire? There were such women out there.

The elevator door opened, a few people came out, and Winona and Ron walked in. Two other men followed them on. Winona and Ron stood by each other, hands held in front of them.

"Nice day out today, isn't it?" Winona said. After all,

they were both people; there was no reason they couldn't simply speak to each other.

"It is, it is," said Ron, coughing into his black glove.

The two men got off on the 43rd floor, and Winona and Ron were alone again.

"This elevator goes so fast," Winona commented.

"Yes," Ron said, giving her a peculiar look, as if the speed of elevators were insignificant.

Winona smiled again, a pressure building up behind her forehead. She was nothing—really, truly nothing—to him.

•

Rex was on the phone when she got to the office, but when she turned on her computer, a little envelope blinked at the bottom of the screen.

Dear Winona, Would the Princess of Writing Implements and So Much More be interested sometime next week in having a friendly but not too-friendly lunch with me, Scribbler of Repetitive Documents? We could meet in the lobby: I'll be wearing a fedora and sunglasses. You'll be under a yellow umbrella. — Rex

Winona stared at the message, alarmed. Something about it hurt her.

Carefully, she wrote back: Implement to Scribbler: Sounds good, maybe pizza?

And she persevered through the day, working with Sandy on new job descriptions for Nancy and Lucy; studying files that Bill said she'd need, doing the regular amount of in-box emptying. Avoiding Nancy, for obvious reasons, and Rex, for reasons a little less clear.

At lunch, the buildings looked lopsided and there

was a peril to the shadows. It was a cold March day and her sunglasses felt sharp on her nose and forehead as she walked block after block. Her body was lost somewhere in her coat and her movement.

She'd had sex with Sylvester, it was true. It hadn't been exactly revelatory. But everything felt stirred up, like a dust storm, and she couldn't see where she was going. As Winona walked, she instructed herself in the responsibilities of the artist. Even this: you could film this feeling.

•

Or you could film something more mysterious, more beautiful.

It was dark outside and the office had quieted down when Winona took her new video camera out of its black bag. This camera, $734.56 including tax, was the embodiment of . . . something. She ran her hands over it, like running her hand over the future, then pulled out the viewfinder and turned the camera on standby. She looked up toward the conference room when the thing buzzed and clanked, setting itself into position. Sandy didn't hear anything, Winona was sure. She was immersed in her phone conversation.

Winona stole into the conference room and pressed the record button. Sandy's shoes and ankles, then the bookcase, and then Sandy on the phone with her computer in the background came into focus, reeled first left and then right in the display monitor.

The automatic light went on and hit Sandy's blond hair like a beam. In the small TV, Sandy appeared touched by something otherworldly. Her mouth spoke but in the frame her words were lost. The grasshopper angle of her knees and ankles, that was something, and the instinct revealed in her shoulder: to be human, like the rest of us.

Sex

In which Winona is tied up by a tawdry fiend

1

Winona placed the first letter in front of Sandy and put her finger on the signature line. Sandy touched Winona's finger for a fraction of a second, put the pen's tip there and signed her name, the S's swirling like twin snakes. Winona took that letter and placed another in its place. Held her finger there. Sandy touched her.

Again, they repeated the process.

"I talked to Sylvester yesterday," Sandy said. "He said you're a nice girl."

"Oh, joy."

"You be careful with him, okay? He's just like all the boys."

"Oh, it's easy to be careful with him," said Winona. After all, they never actually spoke or saw each other.

(Well, it had been a week—but a week of silence after a liaison like theirs may as well be twenty years.)

"We'll have to go out again sometime," Sandy said. "I love that restaurant we went to, though I don't know—maybe just the two of us this time?"

"That sounds great—definitely a step above my normal fare."

"Just give me a couple of weeks, after this Palm business settles down."

They had gotten to the bottom of the stack of letters. Winona picked up the smooth ivory papers and knocked them straight on the table. She held them in her lap and looked over at Sandy and smiled. It was hard not to smile, even though Winona knew Sandy couldn't see her. It seemed right to do it anyway, like she had a belief in Winona, and Winona was following through.

Sandy said: "Listen, would you mind taking this small packet to an associate of mine? I'd use the messenger service, but you know what? Half those people are on crack. For this, I really need someone I can trust."

"I'm always looking for a reason to get out of the office."

"Just don't take this as an invitation to go to a matinee or whatever you filmmakers do in your spare time."

"I would if I could," said Winona. "Research, you know? That's what we call it."

Sandy was beautiful today, as always. Her violet lipstick shimmered in contrast to the moody blue of her blouse. She leaned down and slipped a brown envelope out of her briefcase and handed it to Winona.

Winona felt the necessity of her job. She was proud of

what she did. Whatever would make it good, easy, satisfying for Sandy, Winona could do it for her.

•

Envelope in hand, Winona walked down Fifth Avenue. The sun was shining and she had unzipped her jacket. Even with her sunglasses, she could hardly see, it was so bright. Light/dark: Winona thought she could work with that in *The Anxiety of Everyday Objects,* though she wouldn't want to be too obvious, of course. Obviousness was frowned upon, yet then again so was the oblique. There was some kind of wondrous middle ground, and she could use it, that sense of a middle ground, the steep fall-off on either side, because it mirrored the anxieties of her heroine, she of the sensory-deprivation site, the laps into the shallow and the deep, the world of Big Cups.

There was something about vodka shots with Sylvester, the spinning glass snow geese, which had seemed romantic to Winona, bittersweet and beautiful in a way she couldn't define. There were the whirling birds, and then there was her own slight spin, the feeling that she was falling, as Sylvester had pushed her, gently, down. Even film producers are vulnerable as little boys at a time like that, she was thinking, and hope swelled in her, as it had time and again in the days since their tryst in his apartment. His chest had been bare as a Greek statue's. He worked out. It was a good era, the nineties, for even bohemians had begun to go to the gym, so even the dissolute artist would have pecs hard as underwater stones. The bed had been huge. When she sought with one hand a grip of something, she found that she couldn't even reach the edge. The statue had come to life, as if the geese had suddenly alighted, as if blood had surged through marble and made it warm.

It felt alchemical and vaguely unreal. The blood drained out afterward, as she dressed, as he called his car service for her, poured himself another drink. She had been astonished because when she had asked if he would call her soon, although he had not answered exactly, he had recited her number, from memory! It was auspicious.

Still, he hadn't called, and in the time since then she had plunged herself into her work, both at the office and with her movie. She was editing her notes. She wanted to develop a treatment, something she could send out. And there was the camera itself. Looking through the lens, something she hadn't done since school, presented Winona with a host of new choices. The camera took away some possibilities, but at the same time offered new, unexpected perspectives on things.

She was closer—an inch closer—to the real world of film, to the secret path separating her from the popcorn-strewn theaters.

Sandy, or the person playing Sandy, wouldn't be the actual heroine; she would be a kind of doppelgänger or counterpart. The real heroine would be going about her business, seeing things, and yet what she *did* see would be wrong half the time, magnified or imagined or skewed—an outburst of her own anxiety. This would be set in contrast to the perfect sightlessness of the blind woman—indeed, her clarity. In the end, it wouldn't be absolutely clear which produced happiness, sight or blindness, but it might be kind of cool to make a certain comment on human nature, vis à vis sight or blindness, regardless.

It did strike Winona, however, that she might need a plot of some kind.

She arrived at the address Sandy had given her and went inside. It was an austere building and no one inside breathed; the receptionist was a confection spun from powder. Winona handed her the package and went back outside. She had thirty minutes left. She walked slowly back to the office, squinting at the people and buildings around her, framing shots, hoping, in the back of her mind, that when she returned she'd find that while she was out Sylvester had called her.

•

But no such luck. Winona got a Diet Coke and, on her way back to her desk, reluctantly stopped at Nancy's office.

"Hi, Nancy."

"Hello, Winona."

"I've been meaning to talk to you about my promotion and all that."

"Ah."

"Thanks for the files."

The day Winona had become office manager, they'd passed in the hall and Nancy had said congratulations and given her a stiff pat on the shoulder. Each morning since, Winona had found single file folders on her chair, as if every night Nancy was handing over the parts of her job, one at a time—never everything, and never spoken about during daylight hours.

"Take what you need," Nancy said.

"Well, titles—it's all one of those newfangled human resource psychology tricks anyway."

"Think so?"

"Sure."

"My title was office manager for eight years."

"Well, we can certainly work together. I'll teach you some things, and you can teach me some things," Winona suggested.

"Ah."

"One thing I do need now is the computer password."

"The computer password?"

"Yeah, Bill told me to get Jason to load one of those complete office systems, you know, with time management software and all that. It will help Sandy. And everyone."

"It's *love*," Nancy said, looking toward the window.

"*Love?*"

"*L-O-V-E*. It will prompt you for your ID, too. Type in *orchid*."

"That's so sweet."

"Sweet, right. I'll remember that."

Winona stood up.

Nancy said: "By the way, Winona, are you aware of the office policy on relationships?"

"Relationships?"

"Yes, relationships. You know."

"I didn't know there was an office policy like that."

"Page eighteen. Look it up some time. An office manager should know these things."

•

Interpersonal relationships that break the boundaries of the professional are strongly discouraged; inappropriate sexual behavior in the workplace is cause for dismissal.

Rex read the passage Winona had marked with a neon-pink Post-It.

"Pretty crazy, huh?" she said. They were at Luigi's Special Restaurant for their promised pizza lunch. Walking down the hall with Rex on their way out together, Winona had glanced in on Nancy. She couldn't help but feel the thrill of mischief.

"Do you think she means us? What a laugh!" Winona continued.

Rex was studying the office manual with extreme concentration. A busboy in a clown costume—some kind of misbegotten publicity stunt, no doubt—knocked down a chair right behind him. Rex jumped.

"Jesus!" he said.

The clown didn't seem to notice this or anything else; he was wearing a Walkman in addition to a red afro wig and a striped clown suit with wilted red ruffles hanging from his wrists and ankles.

"I don't like clowns," Rex said.

"Neither do I, really, although I was thinking of having a clown in my film. Maybe this one. Actually, what I really want is just the soundtrack from an ice cream truck, then a glimpse of Mr. Happy Clown Guy at one point."

"Wasn't the ice cream truck ditty/psycho murderer theme already played out in some movie?"

"I don't know, was it?"

"Peter Lorre, maybe. I think it was *M*."

"I better rent that one. But anyway—what about Nancy?"

"If you want a clown in your movie, you could always have me."

"You? Rex, you'd be the hero, if anything."

They both thought about their date then. Winona thought about it and ejected it from her mind like a clown on a high wire jumping headlong into nowhere; Rex thought about it like a clown, too, but his was clinging with red-gloved hands to the safety net underneath.

"Oh, thanks a lot, I believe that one." He started shaking pepper flakes onto his slice in a desultory manner. "Then again, all the old themes keep coming back. Love, death. They're always kicking the same old dead horses. Poor horses."

"C'mon Rex, focus."

"She probably read our e-mails. I bet that's it."

"Our e-mails? That's not right."

"It might not be right, but it's possible."

"Well, I don't have anything very interesting in my e-mails."

"Yeah, right."

"Got enough pepper there, sport?"

"Huh? Yeah."

They were silent for a minute.

"I'll be working here pretty soon, when all this is over," he said.

"When all what's over?"

"It'll be Grecko Mauster Crill *Spires*, not *Willard*, like in dreams of yon. Yore?"

"Oh, yeah? Sandy? She's really amazing, isn't she? Who knew that a blind woman would be so—so daring, so visionary."

"Don't get too entranced."

"Oh, I'm not."

"I mean, it's like she's wooing you or something.

Lunches, fancy ladies' days out, promotions. Film producers."

Winona shrugged. "It's no big deal, believe me."

"I wonder if Nancy has really been looking at our e-mails, Winona. How ironic to be caught by the flower lady. Caught at nothing, I might add. But still, we should be careful. You know how flower ladies can be when they're angry."

"I know. They start putting potpourri in your hard drive."

"Yeah, or laminating *Have a Happy Day* on your forehead."

"Well, we'll have to be careful," Winona said, somewhat doubtfully. Nancy was wrong, so wrong. What a wanton disregard for the obvious.

"It's hard enough to scale to the heights of my career *without* irony," Rex was saying, almost rambling to himself. "I was looking for simple days. You, me, the golden retriever. The porch and the can of cold Budweiser. But maybe artists don't think that way."

"True, we're more the weimaraner-and-sherry types. But the porch would work out all right."

•

Yes, the golden retriever and the porch were in his dream. He hadn't made that part up. It went along with the whole idea of the philosopher-gentleman-lawyer and the gardener-filmmaker-mom with a straw hat and a camera. The Budweiser he'd thrown in just to be funny.

Rex stared out his window at the next building. The windows bounced back blank, like a cop's mirrored shades.

When he was a kid, Rex got a Lionel starter kit one

Christmas. He was attracted to the wheels, the gadgety connectors, and, most of all, the throttle: light and tempting under his finger. But his father was the stationmaster. That first morning, his dad took things out of the box and started placing rail with rail, train with train, wire with wire. When Rex stuck his pale, pancake-sticky hand in the box, "No!" said his father. And then quieter, "We need to do this carefully, son."

Father and son smiled balefully at each other then and Rex stuck his hands under his shins, bottom rung of the collapsible tower of Rex.

It wasn't until his father left the room that Rex grasped the power box and switch machine in both hands. Sometime in late January, long after the pellets for the engine's smoke stack had been used up or had rolled under the furniture, when they'd taken the tree down and his father had lost interest entirely, Rex brought the trains up to his room and set them up again, alone, and the Willard Line grew passengers and destinations, suffered derailments via Indian ambushes, and had more adventures suitable to toys of the world.

Now, sometimes Rex thought of the train set in a new way. He realized that he hoped to buy a train for a little boy himself someday, his own son. Or daughter—why not? Girls like to travel, too; it was no longer a pink-and-blue world. And it confounded him that while he felt ready (no, *almost* ready) to become a dad himself, he still reeled from the specter of his own father.

It was almost invisible, this subjugation, and he doubted heartily if it were even noticed by anyone but himself. They saw each other here and there, on holidays, or when an occasional case brought his dad into the city. Greg Willard was more or less appeased now—Rex had gone through law school and now here he was, mutual fund and all. Rex sometimes fancied that his father was actually happy with him, or at least satisfied. But sometimes the hook still caught him by the ankle and slammed him down.

A long shadow was descending over the Chrysler Building, that bold silver zone of his livelihood. Bill's scrawl on the Cramer agreement: Rex's interpretation was all wrong; he needed to lean heavily on the fiduciary rather than the moral responsibility of the landowner. Rex knew his argument had been more philosophical than usual, but he'd worked hard on it, and he thought it was ineluctable in its own beautiful, rebel-law way. Yes, he could go back and make the expected argument, which was, he had to grant Bill, foolproof.

But what if he fought him for a change? What if he didn't start sweating like a faucet when Bill cut him down? All the things he'd built—the secure world, the good grades and landing the job at the firm and the three years he'd put in now "paying his dues" and climbing up the ladder (not, actually, up a true *rung* as of yet), and paying his bills on Quicken and really knowing his student loan payment schedule and never being without health insurance—were all right, yes, all very right and good, but also, in some other way, in some parallel universe, all wrong. Rex felt like he was always deferring to someone. So he could get his paycheck. So he could get his education. So he could buy a Kleenex-box apartment in New York for ten years' salary.

He knew it took sacrifices—years of them. He'd seen his father go through it. In the end, you got what you'd been working for. Still, Rex couldn't get his mind to adhere to the idea that progress was taking place. Something about the equation was making him nervous. He'd always felt he needed a plan. But what if the plan wasn't working?

The draft in front of him was messy with blue lines of deletion, scrawled words climbing the margins. He said he'd get it back by five o'clock; he *had* to get it back by then.

Winona. *You'd be the hero, if anything,* she'd said.

And then she'd flipped her hair.

2

T oward the end of the next day, Bill called Winona into his office.

"Close the door behind you," he said.

Sandy was sitting in one of the leather chairs. Her hair was pulled back in some kind of Egyptian clip; today's lip gloss was a shade brighter than usual.

"Love that barrette," Winona said, sitting down in the other chair.

Sandy reached up and touched the gold. "Thanks, Win. Bloomingdales."

Mauster looked at one, then the other woman.

"Huh-chu-hum," he uttered. "Now, Miss Bartlett, you've been the office manager for, what, a week?"

"Something like that, Mr. Mauster."

"*Something* like that? Does this mean you've been treating your new position lackadaisically?"

"It was Wednesday, right? I don't have the exact date, though if I looked at my calendar—"

"Unnecessary. But you know, these sorts of things need to mean something, don't they, Sandy? Miss Bartlett, you need to grab the ring. You have to embrace your power."

"Winona," said Sandy. "Bill's right. What he's getting at is that you've got responsibilities now. Lucy is one of them. And she simply cannot, under any circumstances, continue to come in late half the time. This is a law firm, not a charity."

She said *charity* as if it were a dirty word.

"Of course," said Winona.

"She's a good girl," said Bill, a little wistfully. "But it's true, we have too much at stake."

"Tell her if she's late once more, she'll be fired," Sandy said.

"Fired? That's so harsh," said Winona.

"You've got to be aware of where people's skills and flaws lie, without undue concern for allegiances, history," said Bill.

"Can you do this for us?" Sandy asked.

"Well . . ." Winona looked from Bill to Sandy and back. Her job was taking orders: there was no shame in that. She was a team player. Sometimes, if she really wanted to get crazy, she could anticipate what they wanted and do *that* quietly and efficiently. Her new job, office manager, was a far cry from typing envelopes. At least it could be.

"I guess so, if that's what you think is right," she said.

"Fine."

"When do you want me to tell her?"

"Today," Bill said.

"Now," said Sandy.

"Okay, then," Winona said, pressing her sweaty palms against her skirt. "I'll tell her."

"Good," they said in unison.

Winona got up unsteadily and gave Bill a queasy smile. *Embrace your power,* she heard, from a tinny radio in a passing car.

•

There was a woman in India, heir to a dynasty, whose family lost, during the British takeover, everything that had been theirs by blood and centuries-old tradition. They'd been queens and kings, said the article; they'd lived in palaces and banished their enemies. But now they had nothing, nothing at all, yet the old woman lived on, destitute and proud. She was named Queen Mother by her son and daughter; they lived with her in some kind of half-outdoors, half-fallen-down castle, bats and their dozen snarling dogs everywhere. The children begged for food during the day, and they ate the takings from leftover bits of heirloom china. Finally, by drinking a potion that included ground-up royal jewels and pearls, the matriarch committed suicide. Her son and daughter, middle-aged and devoted, embalmed their mother using ancient methods only half remembered—and then they slept by her corpse, brother on the right, sister on the left, until there was almost no more of her. (The embalming didn't work so well after all.)

The story was so bizarre, so impossibly gothic.

Heritage—did it matter? Winona herself felt invisible, neither poor nor rich, nothing in particular. German, Danish, Irish—sure, those were her origins, but her people didn't leap off the page to shake their rights at her, their rights *or* wrongs. She didn't know for sure, but she fairly doubted she came from any German or Danish royalty, and Ireland didn't have royalty, it just had Oscar Wilde and, lately, the seemingly queenly Edna O'Brien.

Winona came from Connecticut. Sometimes when she said that people said *Ohhh* in a knowing kind of way, as if being from Connecticut meant something specific. What *did* it mean? As far as she could tell, it meant you grew up with a dog and a cat, your parents drove VW Rabbits, and your mom always let you get the fancy Jarlsberg cheese at the grocery store.

Dynasty, heritage, strong family feeling—how did these link the past and the future?

The article kept Winona from her distress for about twelve minutes.

She couldn't wait until tomorrow; Lucy could come in late again and be fired without warning. It was almost five o'clock.

It was wrong, but she was going to go ahead and do it anyway. The words in the magazine became hieroglyphics to her.

•

"Hi," Winona said.

"Hi," said Lucy.

"Say, Lucy? You know how I got that promotion and everything?"

"Yes, Miss Office Manager."

"Well, um—"

"What's up, Win? You look paler than usual."

"The thing is, they asked me to talk to you."

"Bill and Umar?"

"Bill and Sandy, actually. They said I should talk to you about being late."

"Oh, yeah?"

"They said—well, they said you have to be on time from now on. If you're late one more time, they might— they said they would—fire you."

Lucy sat back in her chair, placing her hands on her thighs. She stared at Winona for a moment before speaking.

"Winona, you know why I'm late sometimes. Denzel, my mother. You know all that."

"I know."

"I'd like to say I'll never be late again, but I don't think I can make that promise. If I come in late, you know I stay late, too. My time cards are always honest."

"I know, Lucy, but Sandy said—"

"If Sandy has something to say, why doesn't she say it herself?" Lucy whispered, leaning forward again.

"I guess because I'm the   "

"Yeah, you're the office manager. But Winona, don't you think it's a little fucked up that they'd send you to tell me this?"

"Lucy, I'm sorry. I know what you're feeling."

"But you don't, Winona. You don't know what I'm feeling."

Lucy broke their gaze first. She started pushing papers into a folder.

Winona stood there for another moment or two, and then went back to her desk.

Waiting for a last letter to print, Winona looked through the Mr. Ed window to the conference room, where Sandy was tapping away at something. The sky had a violet cast, like a dusty plum. Somewhere out there was the Manhattan grid, cars and people all slow and dumb from up here. Somewhere also was their own patch of the Hudson, and, standing upright and watchful, pale green in the dissolving light, the Statue of Liberty.

Lucy was already gone when Winona left for the day. This was unusual; Lucy usually said good-bye before she went. Sometimes they walked down to the subway together.

Winona went home alone. On her way back to her apartment she bought a take-out dinner at her favorite Polish diner on First Avenue—not a big meal, just mushroom soup and a couple of slices of rye bread with butter. If she ate too much at the end of the day, she felt weirdly lonely. She'd be too full to do all the productive things: little errands, little chores, little improving schemes involving reading and writing. She smiled ruefully to herself, waiting for her order: she and Jeremy came here sometimes, or used to, anyway. She wondered if it was too early, or just too stupid, to give him a call, just to see how he was doing.

When she got back home, she always checked her phone message machine first thing. It said *0*, like a tiny halo on nobody.

•

Maybe she just had to get out of her head. Maybe, after being released from celibacy by Sylvester, she felt, well, released. Or maybe Winona was bored. There is a kind of anger that feels, in polite people, most of all like torpor. In any case, when the phone rang, and it was William—her old pal William—there was something about him that sounded good, alive, to her.

"What are you doing right now?" he asked in a sultry way.

She had always liked William's voice. He was a tall guy, tall and very thin, and he had black hair that fell in a swoop over his eyes . . . at least it used to. At NYU, he was the furthest thing from a ladies man that you could imagine. He let his hair grow out too much before cutting it and had forgotten to shop for clothes in this century. But there was something about him that was appealing. One cool thing was that he wrote all night. He started at midnight and went to bed when the sun came up. This made him seem like a bona fide outcast from ordinary life.

William also had this peculiar relationship with sex: he masturbated with Olympic vigor and frequency and generally thought about sex all the time, and in all that thinking he never seemed to believe sex could possibly be any deeper or more complex than brushing your teeth. It was just something you had to do and, hey, if you did it with someone else, so much the better, in terms of efficiency.

They had never really broken up, only drifted apart, as casually as they'd come together in the first place, two semi-bored students stroking each other's jeans in the back of Documentary 2.

"I'm just hanging out, William. What are you up to? Are you in town?"

"I'm at my brother's apartment. I'm staying here for a couple of weeks, taking care of some business. But right now I'm so horny and lonely, it's unbelievable."

"William, we haven't talked in months and you call and tell me within ten seconds that you're horny?"

"Yeah. And getting hornier."

"You're amazing," Winona said. Despite herself, something was happening to her body.

"Can I come over?" he asked.

"No."

"Please?"

"I'm busy tonight, but some other time."

"Can you just talk me through it? What are you wearing right now?"

Winona looked down at her sweatshirt and jeans and pink socks. She looked over at her little table, the one by her closet, where she lit three votive candles every night. The fire made her feel like something was going on in her tiny, empty studio, that it wasn't just her and Fruit Bat, but rather her, Fruit Bat, and the mighty elements.

There seemed to be some kind of relief in what he was offering.

"Well, William, I'm not really wearing very much at all," she said tentatively.

"You're not?"

"No. Just this little, oh, what do you call it."

"A negligee? Some lingerie? A little dainty feminine nothing?"

"No. It's like this little, this little fireman's outfit."

"Really? Oh, I like that. Like a hat, and some red hotpants?"

164

"William, this is crazy."

"No, no, no."

"Can't we just talk about something else, like what you've been up to career-wise? Don't you want to know about my screenplay?"

"That kind of stuff, Winona—that's for other people to care about. Clueless mortals. I don't give a shit about your career or my career. I just want to—this is really, really getting out of control. How about if you tell me what you are feeling right now. I want to know about your body. Every bit of it. Every inch. Every morsel. What are you doing with your hands right now?"

She stared at the candles.

"My hands?"

"Yes."

"My fingers?"

"Yes."

3 〜

Winona had three red and five green M & M's lined up on her computer. M & M's were a reward system she'd developed to accelerate her progress through her in-box. She got one per page of typing. It was pretty pathetic. Today she felt questionable to horrible about typing, among other things. These were the very last eight M & M's she was going to have. Ever.

Sandy handed her a disk through the Mr. Ed window and leaned in casually, like she was drinking a margarita at a seaside bar.

"You know," Sandy began. "I am more and more impressed with Bill. He knows the right moment to strike. There's nothing so gratifying as being in the presence of a powerful man at his finest hour, when all his intelligence and intuition is aimed at a problem, and he pulverizes it with the fierceness of his stare. It's erotic. Do you want to know my definition of seduction?"

"Sandy, I'm cutting off your coffee supply."

"Seduction is when you know there will be only one answer. One. What is the answer?"

"I guess that, well—"

"The city will fall. The crop will come up. The medicine will be found. The case will be won."

"Gosh."

"*Yes* is the answer. There's no chance of failure. Isn't it invigorating? They talk about restraint and release—for me, it's only *yes.* You will succumb. There's nothing, nothing, as sexy as confidence."

"Right . . ." Winona said.

"On the other hand, an adversary—or a lover—needs to find the way in. If it's money he wants, or power, that's where to go at him. For some men, it's sex itself. See, a woman needs a way in. To succeed, you need to find the chink."

"The chink?"

"In the armor. The weakness, Winona. Usually mixed right in with the strength."

Before Winona could respond, she saw Rex standing in the hallway entrance.

"Are the interrogatories ready yet?" he asked in a peculiar voice.

She had avoided him all day—kept out of the storage room when she knew he was in there getting a cup of coffee, stayed on the phone when he was dropping things off in her in-box, looked the other way when she walked past his office door. Last night's phone call was still on her fingers. So what? Big deal. But when she looked at Rex she felt like she was facing some kind of moral barometer. And now he'd also heard this talk from Sandy, risqué and intimate.

Still Rex looked at her with a calm expression, waiting.

"Almost," she said, smiling quickly, then looking away.

•

Winona walked up front later and asked Lucy if she wanted some coffee. No thank you, Lucy said, without looking up. She had been there, primly collating, when Winona arrived that morning. Winona left her alone, again, chastened by the precision of her speech.

Shush-shush-shush said the photocopier, and Winona was staring, as she usually did when making copies, at the poster detailing the Heimlich maneuver. Why this was in front of the photocopier was not really clear. Still, she studied it more attentively than usual. Perhaps if Lucy choked, and Winona was able to wrest her single-handedly from the fury of death, none of this would matter.

"Bastards!" she heard from the front hall.

She went out to investigate. Lucy was peering over the reception wall; Umar, returned from court, dragged his briefcase full of spent legal documents like a bow-case or scabbard.

"Scoundrels!" he howled.

"What happened?" Winona asked as Umar slumped down onto the couch and ran his hand through his curls.

"Yes, what happened? That's a very good question, Winona. Well, it turns out that Mr. Gregory, formerly of Arkansas, formerly of California, formerly of Alaska, is actually not a U.S. citizen at all, but has been using his cousin's name and history this whole time. It's *Gerald* Gregory, not Jeff Gregory, as it turns out. And Brawnship meets us at the door with this information—like she couldn't get it to us sooner—and what do you know, there's Mr. Gregory I and Mr. Gregory II, sitting polite as you please right next to each other in court. *Our* Mr. Gregory is handcuffed and there's an INS agent smiling like a lunatic. So when it comes to proving him innocent for the little embezzlements he's been surrounded by these past few years, it's a little difficult because now we're faced with not only his lies but the fact that the whole thing is goddamned moot, and he's about to be deported. Back to Zimbabwe or whatever spear-chucking country he came from."

After a pause, Winona said: "I think it *was* Zimbabwe, Umar. But I don't think anyone's actually chucking spears."

"Right, sure."

"Well," Winona continued, gathering a certain degree of momentum. "Mr. Gregory certainly was clever to get all those documents with photographs and signatures. I wonder how many of our clients aren't who they say they are."

"No one is who they say they are," Lucy said ominously.

"True," Winona agreed—though in retrospect she was unsure whether she herself was implicated here.

A tiny old man opened the door like he was pushing a boulder away from the mouth of a cave, and then came shuffling forward.

Winona stepped up to him and shouted: "Hello, Mr. Jibbs, how are you today?"

He held up a letter. "This came in the mail. Don't know what to make of it."

She looked at the crumpled notice from the tax assessor.

"Already sent them the money," the old man wheezed.

"Oh, yes," said Umar, scrubbing his head like he was shampooing his hair. He stood up and put out his hand. "Hello, Mr. Jibbs."

Mr. Jibbs lived in Umar's building, in a rent-controlled apartment he'd held on to for thirty-seven years. He'd seen much of his retirement income disappear through mysterious bureaucratic processes.

"Already sent them the money," Mr. Jibbs repeated.

"Yes, I'm sure you did," said Umar, putting his arm around the older man's thin shoulder. "Why don't we go to my office and take a look?"

"I told them, when they called, that Mr. Crill could help. Mr. Crill knows what you thieves are doing to me!"

"Yes, sir," said Umar, steering him down the hall.

"Bastards! Thieves!" the old man rasped, and Lucy remained motionless, staring at the door.

Back at her desk, Winona started an article on the aerodynamics of feathers. It seemed the military was creating planes with wings simulating the industrious grace of a red hawk's tail, its resilience and pliability, the fronds that all together create a long narrow sheet of gentle resistance. It was the kind of thing a younger Winona ought to have known when she was practicing high jumps off the neighbor's stone wall. Back then, she padded around the yard toe-first like an Indian: she'd read about that somewhere. Fashioning a flying shirt with feathers would have been a good second step to full-throttle interaction with her environment.

When she was an Indian and a wall-jumper, there was no office hierarchy to negotiate. The key to success wasn't written in invisible teletype; instead it was a simple matter of keeping your eyes and ears tuned to the angle of the ground, the direction of the air.

4 ∽

*S*ylvester called on Tuesday, right after work. Did she want to have a drink? If so, perhaps they could meet at his office. She could easily read into his voice any quantity of apology and desire.

Winona got off the phone and threw open her closet. Some strange Cosmo-girl urge came over her, and she put on a miniskirt. She wanted to look good. She wanted him to know that for two whole weeks he'd been missing something.

She took the L across town and walked the rest of the way slowly, enjoying the twilight and the gait her clunky boots forced. She felt like an anti-feminist. What made her feel that way? Wanting to be looked at? You look at rock stars, at presidents, at bishops. God knows they aren't looking back.

She rang the bell at the street and he buzzed her in. The stairwell echoed with her steps. Then she heard the clanking of a deadbolt slipping out, a chain being undone.

"Hello," he called.

"Hi," she said. She was unfortunately out of breath. It didn't help her to convey herself as casual and relaxed.

She walked past Sylvester, standing tall and animalistic by the door, and stopped in the middle of the room. The walls were caramel-colored, a kind of faux-marble paint job. The floor was sleek and clean. In front of the window sat a wide wooden desk with a phone and an answering machine on it. A lamp with a hanging tasseled shade occupied one corner, a knee-high refrigerator the other.

"It's all so—so empty," she said.

"We have stationery. We have business cards."

"Yes, but, I don't know. Don't you have cameras or projectors or screens? Or even the traditional casting couch?"

Sylvester had his hands in his pockets; he was watching her.

"We have a view of a packing plant."

The light was astonishing, actually. The lampshade, an inverted tulip, gave off a warm, almost candlelike aura, and the big windows were bright with dusk.

He stooped by the refrigerator and pulled a bottle out of the freezer.

"Want a martini? I'm hungry for olives."

"Sure," Winona said—it beat broccoli and seltzer.

She watched him bring the bottle and a jar over to the desk. He sat down and opened a drawer, pulled out vermouth and glasses. His clothes were cashmere and linen and were layered with careful disregard.

She felt that she knew what was going on because she had a guidebook and binoculars. It was like being in a foreign land: there was the koala, and there was the rattler. She felt this word: *single*. She felt this word: *unattached*.

He took a first sip and stared ahead, comfortable.

"Cute skirt," he said.

"Thanks."

He looked at her, then looked back down.

Maybe words weren't really right for them. It almost seemed that language might be irrelevant, perhaps even harmful to the perfection of the moment. Still, Winona felt compelled to speak.

"I got a camera," she said.

"You did, huh? Going to make the great American film?"

"Well, yeah."

He shook his head and took another sip of his drink. "Everyone's got a film in them these days."

"What about you? Did you ever make your own films, before you decided to be a producer?"

"Oh sure, I've held the camera."

"What were they about?"

"This and that."

"Like what?"

He put his glass down and stretched, as if suddenly, lazily exhausted. "Did I mention that's a cute skirt?"

This time he ran his finger along the hem.

"Hey, you're changing the subject."

"I don't want to talk about it."

"I talked about my movie. You can't let me be the only fool who wants to be sincere around here."

"Sure I can."

They were just joking around, she imagined.

"Well, that's okay, I guess. Some people don't really like to talk about their work."

"I made a film about a kid who finds the perfect woman for him, the very perfect woman, so beautiful, so mysterious, and then he loses her. And he spends the rest of his life searching for her in the bars and alleyways of Morocco, but all he finds are shadows and ghosts of what had been. At the end, he dies, alone, broken-hearted, staring at her photograph, a glass of eau de vie in his fist."

"Wow, Sylvester. That sounds . . . dramatic."

"It's the story of my life."

"It is?"

Sylvester got up and walked back to the refrigerator. He got out the vodka, then meandered back to the desk.

"You're such a beauty, and so young," he said, touching her face, then kissing her.

•

The next day Winona bought a hat on her way to work. It was a black crocheted cap with a rolled brim pinned up on one side with a huge cloth daisy. She didn't actually think anyone would like it. Her sister would think it "funky" (Liz's nomenclature for anything she thought better suited to college students than Bartletts); her mother would consider it bizarre; and to the lawyers in the firm it would be frippery and nonsense. Although Rex, Rex might like it. Not that she cared what he thought.

Sylvester, he didn't notice things like hats. He was an artist, but on a different level. Something like that. Winona sighed. When she woke up that morning, she'd felt like a faded starlet, a faded starlet keeping her chin up. She needed a cigarette holder, a run in her stocking, a smudge of eyeliner. To counteract that feeling she'd brought her camera to work.

Lucy chuckled and shook her head. "That hat's something else, Winona."

"Thank you, Lucy," Winona said, tentatively, still frightened by how polite Lucy had been lately, how thoroughly she'd been straightening her desk. "I got it from a street vendor."

"I never would have guessed."

Winona took off her jacket and draped it over her arm.

A client file, bulging on both sides, lay on Lucy's desk. Lucy slid apart the long metal fastener and proceeded to slip in a new letter.

"So how's it going, Lucy?"

Lucy shrugged. "Fine."

"You've been getting in before me every day. You should be giving me a hard time about that."

"Hey, I've been lucky for a few days. Although frankly, after that Zimbabwe conversation, I didn't feel like coming in at all."

"Zimbabwe conversation?"

Lucy squinted at her. "Yeah."

"Oh. You mean Umar?"

"Yes, Umar. And of course, everyone pretty much let it slide."

"Yes. Spear throwing, right?"

"Don't remind me."

"Lucy, you know Umar gets away with that type of thing all the time."

"Yeah—because nothing, no one, stands in his way."

"Yeah," Winona said. Her forehead pulsed; the hat felt too tight. "But what can we do?"

"Uh—stand up for what's right?"

"True, but—you didn't say anything, either."

"I could get really sick of being the only black woman in the room who has to say, 'Oh, excuse me, but that's a racist comment.'"

"I can see that. That's a bad situation."

Lucy chuckled. Her curls fell over one side of her headband and across her cheek.

"What?"

"Your expression."

"My expression?"

"You look like you were born yesterday. Didn't you ever skin a knee when you were a child? Didn't your mother ever hit you when it wasn't your fault?"

"Yes, I mean, no, but—"

"Listen kid, the world *is* a treacherous place. Sorry to break the news to you at this late date. How old are you again?" Lucy asked. "Anyway, you're my girl—my Girl from Connecticut. Stay as you are. Sure, why not?"

Winona stood there in her hat with the daisy and the jaunty brim and her hair at odd angles, dismayed by Lucy's description of her, unsure what to do next. Rex rounded the corner.

"There she is," he said, sounding a little faded himself. His glance was too fast for her to register, then he was winging a letter into the mailbox on the counter.

Next, Nancy appeared.

"Oh, hello," she said. She leaned on the reception wall with one hand, took off her high-heeled shoe and started shaking something from the toe. "I'm so glad everyone's together. This might be a good time for me to mention the content of a memo I'm about to distribute. You see, I feel we still have serious compliance issues on the filing of time reports from all the attorneys and—"

"Nancy, can we come back to this?" Rex said, interrupting her. "I've got major work to do. Major."

"Oh," Nancy said, with resounding civility. "Of *course*. This can wait. Sure."

She put her shoe back on, straightened herself, and swept them all with a glare.

•

At noon, Winona took off for lunch, her camera bag on her shoulder. Now she was lurking—like Jean Cocteau, like Luis Buñuel—on the sidewalk, her finger on the Record button, her eye on the Chrysler Building's bank of glass doors.

People moved like two races were going on, one back and one forward. Then there she was, coming out the door. Her stick first, then the rest of her. Winona turned the camera on. The figure in the monitor found her way into the crowd, stepped into the current. Now she stood at the curb to hail a taxi. Ten feet back, Winona stood, her heart beating strong, and zoomed in on Sandy's unsmiling face, her hand making magic in the air.

The screen washed with yellow and Sandy disappeared.

•

Days and nights passed and Sylvester, once more, had vanished. She imagined his phone ringing in the empty office. Sometimes she imagined him there, listening. Then William called her.

"Winona, I'm on the corner of First and Houston with a box of cannolis and a six-pack of the good stuff. Can I come over?"

William, William, William. Good old William. Should she have him over? It would be like renting the sex machine in *Sleeper*.

5 ~

Winona sat on the loveseat and bit into a cannoli. William leaned on the counter.

"So, what's up?" he asked.

"Nothing much. Working on my screenplay."

"Yeah?"

Pause.

Winona said: "So, tell me about California, Tinsel Town and all that."

"It's there, it's happening. I'm working some connections. A friend of mine is writing for *Seinfeld*. I've got some possibilities."

He looked at her from underneath his black wing of hair.

"Cool," Winona said.

"Yeah," he shrugged again. "Hollywood. Way fucked up."

"Really? How so?" He'd always wanted to go directly there. They'd had arguments about selling out, Winona being the hold out for the un-lucrative and bizarre.

"Well, people like us, you know, with MFAs and Big Dreams? We're the minnows on which they feed. Walk down Hollywood Boulevard and you can see the remains of all the Filmmakers with Big Dreams on the pavement, chomped up little arm and leg bones. They use finger bones for toothpicks. The brains are run right over by the fucking Lexuses and Rolls-Royces."

"Sounds lovely."

"But I'm going to show them. I will. I know you don't believe me."

"Sure, I believe you, why not? You've always had a lot of talent."

He scoffed. "Talent isn't even worth pennies in Hollywood."

"Well, let's drink to the demise of talent."

They sat on the little couch and sipped their beers. He started crawling his fingers up her pants.

"Stop that," she said, swatting him.

As soon as his hand was pushed back, it returned. Pretty soon she just held her palm flat over her crotch, the final frontier, and he spun his hand this way then that way around her legs.

"I haven't had sex in *soooo* long," he lamented.

"Really?"

"Let's go to bed," he whispered hoarsely. "Seriously."

"No, we can't," she said.

"I know how to please you."

"William, I don't feel like it."

"Oh, okay," he said. A minute later he insinuated a finger between the buttons of her shirt.

She did pull away. She did. But it took longer than it should have.

Fruit Bat watched from on top of the television. He'd basically seen it all. He'd seen them come and go, had sniffed cigarettes and German shepherds and country air and gasoline on the cuffs of jeans, pressed chinos, tight Brit-twit/Rod Stewart leggings. Usually he just ignored the event. For nine years now, his little brown-gray meals came like clockwork regardless of what strange compulsion for company had taken over his heroine.

Still, if things got really bad, he'd hop into the closet and huddle between her shoes, riding out the invasion.

•

Winona brought Bill his coffee the next morning, setting it on his green blotter. She cast a look at his granddaughter, feet in the sand. Female innocence, framed in silver. The kid was probably great. Most kids were.

"Having a good day so far, Mr. Mauster?" she asked.

Bill looked up. For a moment he seemed to be deciding how to answer, as if she'd perhaps spoken in a foreign language. Then he took off his glasses and leaned, magnanimously, back in his chair.

"Yes, thank you, Miss Bartlett. A good day, a good week. For one thing, I have been pleased to note that Lucy has been on time every day lately."

"Ah."

"'If a man looks sharply, and attentively, he shall see Fortune: for though she be blind, yet she is not invisible.'"

"What?"

He laughed. "Do you know who said that? No? Francis Bacon."

"The painter?"

"The painter? No, dear. What I mean to say is that in important times, everyone, even the least consequential drone, has a role to play. What you do makes a difference. See what I mean? You're working like a team player."

"Thank you," she said, smiling. "Thank you," she said again, hearing the words echo around her.

•

Was it right to admire? Could admiration itself have a flaw? Winona thought Sandy was, well, pretty cool, and she sometimes shone her light on Winona—and then sometimes she just didn't. It was easy enough to attribute this to the requirements of the workplace, but nevertheless it was a little disconcerting. There was still one thing Winona could do unequivocally: she could capture her.

Winona knew Sandy was going out to lunch at one, so she left a few minutes before then and waited in the lobby with her camera.

When Sandy got off the elevator, Winona followed her out to Lexington and then uptown, on foot. Winona began recording.

This time she did get some looks, from people hoping that perhaps she was part of a famous circumstance they could rub up against on their lunch hour. She concentrated in equal parts on the LCD monitor and the path she wove on the sidewalk, twenty feet behind her target.

At the corner of Forty-fourth, Sandy turned. She slowed down—perhaps counting steps?—and then stopped in front of the door to a restaurant. It was a small café with black-and-white checked curtains around the windows and a vast wooden door like the entrance to a rabbit and grog joint from olden days. She went in.

Winona stopped and clicked off the camera. She leaned on the building and let the sun warm her face. After a few minutes, she walked past the restaurant and looked in the window.

She started. Sandy was right there, one table in from the window. She was sitting at a small table, across from another woman. Sandy was talking fast, animatedly. The woman watching her had a tan shawl draped over her shoulders, the kind worn only by the giddy rich or the quaintly infirm. She had brown hair, pressed into obedient curls. Winona tried to discern the relationship: business associate? Friend?

Winona turned her camera back on. She did another walk-by, filming for as long as she could without being noticed, but then she had to put the camera down.

In the lobby at the Hyatt, nestled in between fountains and greenery, Winona played back the images to herself; it was a story she couldn't quite make out. There they were, Sandy, looking almost girlish for a moment, and the woman in the shawl. Then, from under the cashmere shawl, the woman's ballerina hand comes forward and moves across the white tablecloth, wavering for a moment before covering Sandy's own hand. Sandy stops talking. The woman tilts her wrist, curls her fingers into a moon, enveloping what is between. Sandy looks—for the only time Winona can remember—pained. She is staring down. No, she's not staring anywhere. She pulls her hand away, regains something of herself. And it's the other woman's turn to look down.

•

Winona was up front putting the first of three letters from Sandy in the messenger pick-up box when Lucy said "Uh-oh" as she looked toward the door.

In careened Ron Blitzen. His gray topcoat wasn't properly buttoned, the first hint that something wasn't quite on course.

"Hello, Mr. Blitzen," Lucy said.

"Where's Bill? Where's Umar?" he responded, pulling off his tartan scarf as if it had been choking him.

"Just one moment, Mr. Blitzen," said Lucy. "Do you have an appointment?"

"Let me ask you something. Do you need an appointment at the hospital if, say, you've been run over by a *fucking truck*?"

He was leaning over the reception wall. Lucy leaned back.

Winona said: "Mr. Blitzen, have a seat, please, and we'll tell Mr. Mauster you're here."

Ron Blitzen turned around to look at Winona. He smelled of alcohol. His face was sharpened into a sneer. Winona took a couple of steps toward the wall.

"I called three times this morning and no one's returned my call. Three times. Umar's been out, like fucking usual, and Bill hasn't called me back. Why not? You're his secretary. Why not?"

"I'm afraid Mr. Mauster has been very busy today. I'm sure that when he—"

"I don't care if he's busy. He's always busy."

Rex appeared. "What's going on?" he said, placing himself between Winona and Ron.

"Rex, I've got to talk to Bill. We've got some shit going down, Rex. Leo is making some insinuations. He's making some insinuations, Rex. And my wife, Rex. My loving ex-wife, Rex."

"Sir, please sit down—now," Rex said.

Ron gave up, falling onto the couch.

Rex turned to Winona. "Winona, can you get Bill? Thank you."

"That bitch. I *made* her who she is. I made her. That's the thing. And we had dreams together. Dreams," Ron mumbled, more to himself than to anyone else.

"Bill," Ron said as if he'd been surprised out of a snooze when Winona returned with her boss.

Bill said, "C'mon, my friend, let's go in my office and talk. It's all right, everyone. You can go back to work now."

Bill led Ron to his office and closed the door.

"Whoa," Winona said. "I've never seen him like that before."

"No kidding," said Lucy.

"World's going to hell in a handbasket," Nancy said, then went back into her office and closed the door.

"Are you okay?" Rex asked Winona.

"Yeah, I'm fine."

"Lucy, you okay?" Rex asked.

"Oh, sure. Not the first crazy drunk I've ever seen."

"Okay, okay," he said. He just stood there for another second, like a lifeguard out of a job. "Okay," he said a third time, then walked back into his office.

•

In a little while Winona's intercom buzzed. Coffee. That's what Bill wanted.

She had two mugs. She had to place them on the floor while knocking, then open the door, then pick them up again. Ron was sitting on a chair, mumbling something about Leo, wondering how he could have left after all he'd done for him. Bill was on the phone, on hold it seemed. Winona placed the first mug before him, then moved to place Ron's on the desk, but he reached out with his hand. She gave it to him, smiled briefly, politely, and started to leave.

"You're a pretty young woman. Let me ask you something," Ron said all of a sudden.

His eyes were rimmed with red and his lips had a lazy look that had all the wrong connotations. It was, of course, rare for him to notice her presence at all. She felt most of all like running.

"Do you think you could handle perfect happiness? Beauty, money, leisure, fame? The whole thing? In a nice, pretty package?"

"Leave her alone, Ron," said Bill, dropping the phone receiver down.

"No, really, I want to know. Maybe women just don't want happiness after all. Maybe I was wrong. Thousands of women have used Lisa Box. I've got thousands of happy customers. But maybe, maybe—"

"I could handle perfect happiness, Mr. Blitzen," Winona said. "I think most women could."

"So it's just Brenda, then," Ron said, more gruffly than she'd have expected. He looked back at Bill, having dispensed with female wisdom.

"Did I ever tell you what Brenda hated most about herself? Did I tell you that? Get a load of this: her chin. Yes. Her little potato chin. She was obsessed with it. Well, guess what happened after the operation? After I paid thousands of dollars to the best plastic surgeon in Manhattan?"

Ron started laughing, a pitiful, horrible laugh. Winona was staring at his coffee, which was jiggling perilously.

"She started hating her ankles, Bill! Her ankles! See what I'm saying?"

"Let's focus on Stratosphere, Ron," said Bill. "The divorce is a separate matter. It's going to be handled quietly. We need it to be handled quietly. But right now we need to concentrate on the matter at hand." He was as polite as anyone whose firm will go under if a particular case isn't won.

Winona backed out, closing the door behind her. She grabbed her purse and loitered in the snack shop in the basement for as long as possible. Luckily, he was gone when she returned.

•

"Thanks for all your help today, Win," Sandy said, late in the afternoon. "After we got rid of that slug Blitzen, it was hard to get back on course."

For a swift moment Winona thought she detected insincerity in Sandy's voice, and she felt certain that Sandy had discerned, with some kind of fifth or twenty-ninth sense, that Winona had videotaped her earlier.

"No problem," she said.

"You were in there for a while with him and Bill. What were they talking about?"

"I don't know. Bill was on the phone."

"With Doug Sandwitz, the Stratosphere attorney?"

"Maybe. He was on hold."

"Did they mention Lisa's Lil' Sister?"

"Not that I remember. Why?"

Sandy hesitated. "Doesn't matter. Anyway, here, I wanted to give you this."

She placed a small box on the sill between Winona and the hall.

"What is it?"

"Find out for yourself."

Winona picked up the box and lifted the top. "Wow, thanks."

"In the old days you'd get a gold watch when you retired, right? These days you get it as a little graft, mid-career. Anyway, I don't know what they were thinking giving me a watch. That's the last thing I can use, obviously. Now, if they'd made those diamonds into braille, maybe."

"These are real diamonds?"

"Could be. I don't know. They'd better be, is what I'm thinking."

Sandy started walking back into her office.

"Sandy, this is too nice. You can't give this to me," said Winona.

"I can do whatever I want," she said, so gracefully.

When Winona put the watch in her jewelry box at home—she couldn't wear it to the office, and she really didn't want to wear it around the East Village, either—she found herself thinking of it as a real treasure, a tangible embodiment of the connection between herself and Sandy Spires.

6 ⌒

Well, a problem has come to my attention," said Bill. "Yes, Nancy has done her duty as a longtime employee of our firm, a part of our venture, our humble concern, since the very beginning. I remember when she was just out of school, poor thing, couldn't find a job anywhere. But, oh, she could type—and she knew how to organize an office. Probably even before your time, Sandy, we used to have these carbon billing sheets, and she filled them out with her meticulous handwriting."

Sandy nodded. She was standing by the window, smooth in a cream-colored silk suit, her shoes black and sharp.

Rex and Winona sat in the twin chairs before Bill's desk; was it possible the cushions were softer, deeper than usual? Winona felt like she'd sunk down to her neck in leather.

Bill coughed and picked up a piece of paper. He coughed again and covered his mouth with his fist, then put on his reading glasses.

"'Would the Princess of Writing Implements and So Much More be interested sometime next week in having a friendly but not too-friendly lunch with me, Scribbler of Repetitive Documents? We could meet in the lobby: I'll be wearing a fedora and sunglasses. You'll be under a yellow umbrella.'

"Scribbler of Repetitive Documents—that's one way of putting it, don't you think, Sandy?"

She didn't say anything.

"Or how about this," Bill continued, flipping to a new page. *"It's like what I said before—when something like this happens to you, you can't walk away, no matter what. I feel like this might be—'"*

"Okay, Bill—I think you've made your point," Rex interrupted.

Bill peered over his glasses, his forehead throbbing with legality.

"Is this what we've hired you for, Rex?"

"You've hired me to do my job. And I am doing my job, Bill."

"Doing a job on Winona, is what it sounds like."

"He's not doing a job on me."

"See that, Bill? They're innocent as newborn lambs. But guys, why leave a paper trail?" Sandy had her arms folded and was smiling, as if they'd all just come up with a great word combination in Scrabble.

Winona glanced over at Rex. He looked shaky.

"What's the purpose of this meeting?" he said, with obvious anger.

"Oh," Bill said, and leaned back in his chair. "The purpose of this meeting. Well, Rex, the main purpose is *not* to fire the two of you, though that was something we considered. No, it's simply to tell you to keep your mitts off the secretary."

"Bill, she's an office manager," Sandy scolded.

"Okay, keep your mitts off the office manager. And the second thing is this: well, this is pretty obvious too, isn't it? Your time is *mine*. That's what we pay you for, remember?"

Rex hesitated, then said, like he was entering a guilty plea: "Yes, sir."

"Winona?"

"Yes. Right."

Muteness spread over Rex and Winona like the arms of a father.

•

That night Winona took the elevator down to the lobby like usual.

"Winona," Rex said. He was standing in front of the dedication plaque, his hands in the pockets of his trench coat. He was either a lawyer or Humphrey Bogart.

"Rex, what are you doing?"

"Waiting for you. Let's go get a beer."

"Well, okay. I guess we're already busted."

"C'mon," he said, taking her arm.

They crossed the street to Grand Central, hustling along with all the other mad commuters, but then instead of filing out through one of the tall doors to a train, picking up a cocktail for the ride home to Westport, they walked across the lobby and climbed the marble stairs to the balcony. Rex went to the bar and Winona sat at a small round table and stared at the accountants and the secretaries and the doctors and the sales associates.

"Okay, Winona. This is the situation," he said, after he'd placed two drafts on their table and then rearranged the sugar packets. "Something's up at the office."

"Yes. It's Peyton Place, and we're the star attractions."

"Actually, we're not. Sandy is. One night last week I was working late, okay? I saw her and Umar screwing in his office."

"No way."

"I was just looking for the Lisa Box chrono file and so I opened the door. There they were. Up against the wall, to be specific. They must have thought the door was closed, but it wasn't, and I actually thought Umar had left for the day. No one saw me, no one heard me. Umar was—well, facing the other direction. Sandy didn't have her glasses on. It seemed like she was looking at the ceiling, but of course she wasn't looking anywhere at all."

"God, I knew Umar was a big flirt. But still!"

"Well, you know what? I don't really care if Umar and Sandy are having an affair. I don't care at all. But I'm wondering here. You and Sandy—lunches, etcetera. Umar and Sandy—whatever you want to call it. What does she want from you two? Something. She's not doing any of this to pass the time. She's not like a normal person."

"I know she's not normal. I keep telling you that."

"She's unique. She's strange and seductive."

Winona looked at Rex, disconcerted. "Yes, well, so?"

"I can't figure it out. I keep thinking about her."

Winona took a sip of her beer and leaned over the balustrade. There they were: everyone. Where were they going? It seemed like her heroine, the anxious one, was always alone, always watching other people, always listening to her own breathing. It seemed like a stupid idea, really, now that she thought about it. Where was the dramatic arc? The storyline? God, even the indies liked a little point-counterpoint. It couldn't all be thought-thought-feeling-thought. You had to have more than one person in a movie, is what she was thinking. You can't clap with one hand. If a bear shits in the woods, does a tree fall down?

"Hmm," Winona said.

Rex was sitting there drinking his beer and looking at her, like it was her turn to come up with something.

"What do you mean, she's seductive?" she said. She had a headache. She wanted to go home.

7 ∽

If this were a detective movie, now would be when the promising lead turns into a dud. Grecko Mauster Crill, which had always been—even on its most difficult days—a place where Winona felt she could hide in a fugue of manners, hazy as pantyhose, was beginning to feel dangerous.

She felt betrayed by Sandy. They weren't lovers, obviously. Still, she'd thought they'd had a unique connection—a girl thing, something that had to do with smoking on benches and being beautiful together. (The image of Sandy at the restaurant, the knowledge that she, too, could be touched by someone, made the possibility seem even more real.) But sex against the wall with Umar kind of blew it out of the water.

Now Rex seemed to be withdrawing, like a Cheshire cat, disappearing from the world.

There was no *absolutely* tangible reason to believe this. But there had been the advent of certain new equations: Sandy=seductive. Sandy=can't stop thinking about her. And since that day, a kind of hardness or remoteness in Rex that Winona couldn't put her finger on.

Winona took a series of actions: first, she threw out all her magazines. (It *was* going a little overboard.) She did hyper-useful things at work the rest of the week, like making all the verb tenses in the job descriptions parallel and generating an inventory sheet for ink cartridges. This productivity lasted through the weekend. By Sunday, she had ironed everything she owned and reorganized her closet by shade and season. She'd done all her hand-washables and was sewing buttons on an ancient skirt (and swatting away Fruit Bat, who attacked the needle every five seconds), when the buzzer rang. It was William. She let him in.

"I'm leaving tomorrow," he said, sitting on her loveseat.

"I knew it was soon. Well, it's been fun having you around."

"You won't miss me, will you?"

"Of course I'll miss you, William."

"If I stayed, we could get married, have some kids, buy a little house in the country."

"Sure we could."

"I'd take a full-time job selling window treatments. No, I'd have two jobs. You wouldn't have to work. I'd take care of you. All you'd do is stay in bed all day, filing your nails and reading *The Wizard of Oz* to our progeny."

"I can hardly restrain myself."

"Ah," he said and jumped up. "That's exactly what I wanted to hear!"

"What?"

He put his arms around her and then started pawing her—not polite, but not threatening either.

"I want to restrain you," he whispered into her ear.

"I already feel restrained enough, thank you."

"Yes, that's the thing, see? I can do you a favor. I can release you from your commonplace bonds. You just have to trust me. *Trust me*," he repeated.

William put his hand in his pocket and came up with two black satin sashes. He held one in each hand and twirled around like he was auditioning for the role of savior.

"William, this isn't your thing. You're weird, but not, you know, a gadget person. Are you into S & M now?"

"Oh, 'S & M'—that's just terminology. Anyway, *this* isn't *that*. I'm just thinking it would be amusing. To be honest, I found these in my dad's sports bag and I don't know what the fuck they're for. Maybe they're for tying tetherballs to poles. Who fucking knows? But the thing is, Winona, just for me, one little gesture to show that you trust me. That's the thing—see?"

"But—"

"It's not even about sex, see what I mean?"

"Well, that's too bad, but—"

"All you do is sit there. You tell me in advance how far I can go, later, when you are—free."

"You mean like, to first base, or in for a homer? That kind of thing?"

"On the pedestrian level, yes."

He waited, holding his sashes expectantly.

Hey, she was still twenty-nine—technically, *actually,*

in her twenties. And single. And this was New York City, sin city (or was that Las Vegas?). It was the nineties—at the time, virtually futuristic it was so current. She could give it a try, see what it was like, being restrained and everything.

And this had nothing to do with Rex (who was probably at this very moment walking like a zombie toward Sandy's black palace). And it had nothing to do with Sandy herself. She was just a work associate, some girl. Someone Winona typed for. And it had nothing to do with Bill bossing her around and nothing to do with being at a threshold of fierce despair about her film (the camera, which got her closer, only making her taste what she wanted that much more). And nothing, *nothing*, to do with any film producers.

"You can go all the way," she said.

"Really?" he said, sounding surprised.

"Though a condom would be useful, if, well, it comes to that. Does this sort of thing come to that?"

"Anything's possible. Anything at all."

"Okay, then," Winona said. "I'll just hit the john, okay? Then we can get started?"

•

They closed the curtains and put a chair in the middle of the floor.

"Just take off your shirt, for now," said William.

She turned away slightly, pulled her T-shirt over her head. Time had erased the casualness of nudity between them. Given a few months, an ex-boyfriend's gaze becomes strange again, like it has never been otherwise.

She sat down on the chair, her breasts and stomach

bare. He walked behind her and tied her hands to the chair back with the black sash. It was tight but not uncomfortable, perhaps more a suggestion of restraint than restraint itself. Initially, she'd thought he'd be tying her on the bed, she'd seen that in a movie somewhere.

She watched him as he brought the other sash to her face. One minute she was studying his mouth, wondering if they would kiss, and the next she had ducked into a world of black.

"All right," he whispered. "Yes."

His voice was a little tight. She could feel him—she thought she could feel him—leaning close. Under the sash, her eyes were open.

Her shoulders felt bright, like they might be touched. Her breasts, her stomach. She breathed in and out, and then found that she could not do this naturally. She tried not to think about it. She was waiting for him—waiting for him to touch her, to use her. She had no gag in her mouth, but it felt, anyway, like silence was part of this. She waited a little longer.

"You are my slave," he said, then sort of snorted, laughed. That's when she realized he was on the other side of the room.

She laughed, too. It was only William.

He didn't say anything more.

She was colorful, loud. He let her wait a little longer.

The clock was ticking—the downhill acceleration, uphill grind. What would he touch first?

Then she heard him. He was coming closer—she heard his jeans rub. He was behind her. He whispered:

"You didn't miss me last time, either." His voice was like an insect buzzing in her ear.

"What do you mean?"

"You didn't even miss me when I went to L.A."

"What?"

"I was just a convenience. You never even imagined I had a heart to break. What a bitch."

"William, what are you talking about?"

"Bitch. I'm in control now, Little Miss Bitch."

And she heard him walk away. She heard the door to her apartment open, then close.

"William?" she called.

Nothing.

"William?" she said again, softer.

•

She had heard of this, too. Maybe she'd read about it, this kind of thing: a trust exercise. Maybe he was just in the hallway. She rotated her wrists slightly, feeling the tightness of the loop between her body and the chair. He could be pretending to be mad, pretending to be gone.

The clock was ticking and the heater hissed and ticked.

You didn't miss me last time, either. His words still itched in her ear. *Bitch. I'm in control now, Little Miss Bitch.*

Winona heard her own breath. She wasn't exactly hyperventilating, but it could happen if she didn't stop thinking about it. Then the position of her arms came to her like an alarm. They were in a strange and unpleasant triangle. She wanted, more than anything, to move them.

"Fruit Bat?" she called out. He was there somewhere, silent on his black paws.

Was this still part of the thing? Was this, this fucked up feeling, part of the sex thing? Was he coming back? Was she supposed to wait for him?

She remembered Sylvester turning her around against the desk in his empty office. She remembered his shoes, big black fashion clown shoes, splayed out on the wood floor. She was smiling, spinning, acquiescing—

But that wasn't with Sylvester, that was with Bill. That was getting the coffee. Was it the same? It couldn't be the same. Being polite, being nice, was supposed to be a *good* thing.

She tried to pull her hand out, harder this time. How long did she have to wait? William would be disappointed if she untied herself—that would mean she wasn't playing anymore. She should stay. She should wait.

Darkness pulled at her edges. Then they were gone: even her edges were gone. She needed to keep thinking about them, make sure they were distinct. She had to *make* them distinct. This is blindness, then: you don't know where your body is.

Winona felt Fruit Bat's nose on her shin like delicate ice.

8 ⁓

*T*he next morning Winona turned off the alarm. She got out of bed and made a cup of coffee and fed Fruit Bat and took off her nightgown and got in the shower. She shampooed and conditioned her hair, and while the conditioner was in, she shaved her legs. One, then the other, and then her underarms. She dried off, had a few more sips of coffee, had some cereal and listened to classical music on the radio and stood before her closet. In there were the outfits. She would be a secretary today; she would be an office manager—like calling garbage men sanitation engineers. She pulled on her pantyhose. This pair only had one small tear, at the toe. If she put them on right, her toe wouldn't insinuate its way into the hole, making it wider as the day went on, a private noose. She put on her black slip and her demure skirt and her black top with long sleeves and then modest pumps. She spritzed her neck with perfume. She was anyone's version of a normal girl.

Carefully, she left her apartment, locked it, and walked down the two flights of stairs to the lobby of her building, then out the front door.

•

Lucy was on the phone when she came in, writing a message on a telephone pad, patiently repeating a number. Nancy was on the phone, too. Winona could hear Nancy above the scent of her flowers, all seemingly come into riotous bloom. "No, I specifically ordered the files that expanded *two* inches, not four. The four-inch files are much too bulky. They don't fit in our drawers; they wouldn't fit in anyone's drawers. I need the files I ordered and I need them now."

Winona walked by quietly. If she just went about her business.

"Good morning," Winona said, standing in the door to the conference room, where Bill and Sandy were sitting across the table from each other.

"Winona, glad you're here," Sandy said. "We're already at ninety miles an hour. Hope you're prepared."

"Of course."

Bill handed her a draft letter. "This is your first priority. And call a messenger."

"Okay," she said, and turned around.

Winona turned on her computer and placed the pages in the letter holder.

Her wrists stung. If someone saw the marks, she had a story ready: she'd been walking Sniffles and an escaped ferret had raced past them in the lobby. It wasn't a great story.

She held her elbows in close to her body and started inserting phrases: *pursuant to, as we discussed, in accordance with the agreement heretofore ratified,* and nothing made sense to her at all.

Rex came by and dropped something in her in-box.

"Where's *The Wall Street Journal,* you shameless newspaper thief?" he said.

She was struck totally dumb. She couldn't say anything. She just stared at the computer and kept her wrists hidden.

"Winona?" Rex said.

"I've got to get this letter to Bill, Rex. I think the paper is on Lucy's desk."

"Are you okay?"

"I'm fine, thanks," she said. Finally he left.

She'd always thought William was in the relationship for the same reason she was: none, nothing, or at least not much. It seemed that this, in any case, had been understood between them. She didn't know that he apparently wanted, or had once wished for, more, and also that he had a word for her: *bitch.*

But William didn't matter. William was a wisp, a shadow, a total nothing. What mattered was that she let herself get in that position. What mattered was that she thought it would be, if not productive exactly, at least entertaining.

It was like she thought life lasted a really long time and that everything you did didn't matter *utterly,* that you weren't *made* of the minutes you spent.

She took her hands off the keyboard and touched one, then the other wrist.

After she had twisted out of the first sash, she'd pulled the other off her head and her room had come back to her like an old friend and she'd run over to her door and bolted it to keep her life, her own life, in.

•

Winona brought some letters to Sandy for her signature. She leaned over Sandy's desk, near enough for the scent of her perfume to catch in Winona's throat, and put her finger on the signature line. When she reached like that, the burns on her wrists showed, but the blind woman couldn't see that, of course. Sandy brought her pen close.

When the letters were signed, Winona straightened out again, holding the letters by the edges so the sweat of her fingers didn't ruin them.

She remembered being at the salon with Sandy, wearing only white towels, like two children after a dip in the ocean. These were the words that came to mind: *summer friends*. Best friends, and then nothing.

"Sandy, I wanted to talk to you about something," Winona began.

"You don't have to thank me. It was no problem."

"What?"

"Saving the butts of you and your boyfriend."

"Rex?"

"Who did you think I meant?"

"I was wondering, with the trial coming up and everything, if you had ever had a chance, you know, to review those papers?" Winona asked.

Sandy took a moment. "What papers?" she asked, reaching down to turn off her computer.

"The ones I copied for you—discreetly. I just didn't know if you had talked to Umar and Bill yet about Lisa Box, about your ideas for a strategy."

Sandy wasn't looking at her, she was looking toward her. Still, there was a point of recognition, sure as a shared glance, between the two women.

"Not yet, why?"

"Why? Oh, well, I guess I just wondered—I mean, it's been a long time." Winona worried, suddenly, about what she was asking. "I thought you were in a hurry. The trial's coming up and no one's mentioned anything."

"Don't meddle, Winona. Really. Trust me. This is all about timing. You've got to know how men tick, you know?"

Winona got up and walked over to the window. Sandy was putting her tape recorder in her briefcase now, getting ready to leave. Of course, she was just leaving for the day, but Winona was struck by the sense that they were parting forever, standing in black furs on some snow-swept Russian railway, and if she didn't say what she meant, if she didn't get to the heart of the thing –

"You know what you were saying about power and sex, that one time?"

"Remind me."

"You said that power turned you on."

"I never said that."

"You said it about Bill. But I was wondering . . . is the sexy part, for you, being close to the powerful, or being, you know, the powerful one?"

"God, Winona, go ask Dr. Ruth. Don't ask me."

There was an edge to her voice. Still, Winona persevered. She had to make a connection.

"Well, anyway, I did want to thank you for something."

Sandy was latching her briefcase.

"My movie's coming together, that's one thing. I started using my camera."

"That's nice, Winona."

"I've got you to thank—you've made me feel differently about some things."

"Uh-huh, okay."

Sandy picked up her cane from its resting spot on the bookcase and began to walk toward the door. Winona could smell her perfume again, could see her silk blouse rippling.

"I hope you don't mind. I brought my camera to the office a couple of times. I videotaped you. You see, you've been like an inspiration to me, a doppel—"

Sandy stopped before the door. "You what?" she asked, turning around. "First you second-guess my work, then you speculate on my sex life, and then you tell me you've been *filming* me? Without my permission? Are you insane?"

"I should have asked. I'm sorry. If you want it, I'll show you the tape. I'll bring it in tomorrow."

"I can't *see* the tape," Sandy shot back. She stood in the door. She held on to the doorjamb. Then she said: "What was I doing when you were filming me?"

"Well, typing. And also, hailing a cab."

"Typing? What was I typing?"

"I don't know. Nothing, actually. There wasn't anything visible on the screen."

"So that's it? Typing and getting a taxi—that's the sum total of your exciting documentary?"

And there had been the restaurant, that woman, but Winona's sense of self-preservation kicked in.

"Yes, that's about it. Really, it doesn't amount to anything." Winona watched Sandy's face for clues as she considered this. She had replayed the tape so many times, stared at Sandy's image, made it into triangles and squares. "I'm sorry I did it. I didn't mean to make you feel uncomfortable."

"It's not about my feelings, Winona. *Feelings* don't actually come into play."

"The thing is, Sandy, even though we just work together, I feel like I really *know* you."

"You don't know anything about me," Sandy said. She turned and walked away.

•

That evening, Winona discovered that if your dinner consists of a whole pint of chocolate Häagen-Dazs and an airplane bottle of scotch, you get an unbelievable headache. She watched the most amazing set of bad sit-coms waiting for the Tylenol to kick in. Amid domestic crisis number three, the phone rang.

"Hello?"

"Hello," said the voice, and it took her a second to realize who it was.

"Oh, hi, Sylvester," she said, muting the TV. She'd been waiting for this.

"What are you doing?"

At first, she couldn't find the strength to answer. She didn't feel like she was on land—the headache hadn't quite gone away—but she felt that perhaps she was on a sandbar, squinting at the shore. She knew what she had to do. She had learned something by mixing up Sylvester with Bill, William with Sylvester.

"Um, nothing."

"I'm at a bar. I've been thinking about you a lot lately."

Although phone service had gone on uninterrupted in her district, Winona realized, of course, that this wasn't necessarily the case everywhere. A long time ago she'd trained herself—or was it the priest at Sunday school who had done it? or the general Connecticut ethos? or just the outcome of being a girl?—to allow for the fact that a person who does not return phone calls may actually have something quite terrible and stalling going on: they might have discovered they have a deadly disease. They might have been captured by a band of marauders.

"Oh," she finally said, caught between instinct and determination.

"I've been here all night," he said then, sounding as if he were yawning as he spoke.

"You've been at the bar all night?"

"Yeah."

"Oh."

"So, honey, want to come out for a drink?"

Fruit Bat lay in an extensive stretch on the bed by Winona's feet. Winona's own variety of rage, rare and virtually undocumented by science, fluttered in a silvery line somewhere behind her left shoulder.

"Actually, no."

"Tant pis," he said.

"Sylvester, you know, I've been thinking—"

"Can I call you tomorrow, babe? A vast group of young derelicts just descended on me and is seeking to taint my soul with its uncompromising will."

"Well, actually—"

"Tomorrow, my sweet," he said, and clicked off.

"Good-bye," she said. And she knew she meant good-bye for good, and she felt immediately, absolutely giddy.

Innocence ⁓

In which all is revealed

1

Where's Lucy?" Sandy asked, coming up behind Winona. The threads of metal in her dress flashed like needles.

"Lucy?" Winona said, as if that name were unfamiliar. It was 9:20.

"Yes, Lucy. Where is she this morning?" Sandy asked.

"She's not here yet."

"Not here?"

"I don't know what happened. I'm sure it's something understandable. I'll talk to her about it when she gets in."

Sandy stood motionless. "Ah. Well then, can you make these copies for me?"

"Sure."

Sandy turned back toward the conference room.

"I'm sure she'll be here soon, Sandy," Winona said. "I'll be watching for her."

The door closed.

It had been like this for over a week now. "Communication" hadn't been as successful as promised in the couples' conference brochure. Facing the bitchiest Upgrade Panel in Lisa Box history would still beat working in an office with the prickly ire of the blind. Sandy reverberated with meaning, like Christmas morning. Every fax Winona sent was like squeezing her own bones through the chute, every letter was inked in blood, every phone call announced the death of a beloved. When Sandy signed letters with Winona, she didn't touch her anymore.

Winona tried to type softly so she could hear the front door. That didn't work well, so she just got up and loitered around Lucy's desk until, at 9:45, Lucy herself got off the elevator.

She walked in the lobby shaking her umbrella. "Jesus, it's miserable out there. Hey, Winona."

"Hi."

"I thought it was spring already. It's freezing out, and I'm drenched, too. Ever been nose to armpit with a man who fishes for his breakfast in flooded subway tunnels?"

"Lucy, it's quarter of ten."

"So it is."

"Yeah, right. Well, I guess I'll fire you then."

"Okey-dokey."

"No, seriously, Lucy," Winona said. "Sandy's already been asking about you. What's the story? What should we tell them?"

"I don't care," Lucy said, sitting down at her desk and beginning to take off her sneakers.

"You should care."

"I don't care."

"Work with me, Lucy."

Lucy gave Winona a look. "You know what? Some things are private. And sometimes a person needs a little flexibility."

"I'll give you all the flexibility you want, but Sandy's all over me," Winona whispered.

"Winona, the subway was backed up. My mother was late. Same old, same old. I'm sorry. What should I do, beg for forgiveness? If these troglodytes can't understand—"

"Oh. Is this Lucy now?" Sandy said, appearing from the hallway, innocence in her voice.

"Morning, Sandy."

"And good morning to you, Lucy. Winona?"

"Yes?"

"You do recall our previous conversations? About timeliness? Responsibility? The tenets of employment?"

"Yes, but, Sandy, we've got a situation here. Lucy had a circumstance. It's very unusual. And it's not going to happen again. We've spoken about it, and I've got it covered for the future."

"Winona, let's not have two people falling down on the job."

"Sandy," Lucy began, holding her sneaker.

"I have nothing to say to you," Sandy said. "Winona?"

"What?"

"Do your job."

"I'm not going to fire her for this, if that's what you're saying."

"Oh, you're not?"

"No."

Sandy considered this for half a second. "Lucy, gather your things. You're out the door in five minutes. We'll send you your last check."

"Sandy—" Winona said.

"I want someone else sitting at this desk by lunchtime, understood? Needless to say, I'm disappointed in your judgment, Winona. And I'm still waiting for my photocopies."

Sandy turned and walked away.

Lucy didn't hesitate. She took her dress shoes back off and put them in her bag, along with her special mug and her framed photo of Denzel. In the picture, he wore his Little League outfit, holding a baseball and smiling at the camera.

"Lucy, I'm so sorry," said Winona.

Lucy just shook her head and stepped around Winona on her way to the door.

•

Winona went back to her desk. She could hear Sandy in her office, murmuring into the phone. Since when did she have firing rights around here? Was this just something a person picked up, like a dropped handkerchief? Wasn't there some kind of thunderclap or bagpipe ceremony involved? Fuck. Winona had never felt so stupid, so insincere. She typed like a barge moving through frozen waters.

"Happy Secretaries' Day!" Umar bellowed.

Winona turned from her computer and saw that he was holding a basket of pink and yellow daisies.

"I was walking down the street, and I saw the sign in a florist's window. I know it was actually *yesterday*, but of course we'd never forget you, Winona! You deserve the best. You deserve all the flowers any secretary could hope for!"

"Oh, thank you, Umar."

"Oh," he said, suddenly concerned, perhaps noting that Winona was speaking like an automaton. "Have you already gotten a present from us?"

"Oh, no. These are beautiful. Thanks so much."

Winona tried to rally. She held the basket in her hands and admired it for him. How nice: Useless Weakling Appreciation Day. A new Hallmark holiday. She should write them a memo of thanks; the legions of weaklings would finally now get their little funny cards.

"I got a basket for Lucy, too—there's no Receptionist's Day, after all. But where is she?"

"She's been fired."

"What? Fired?"

"She was late this morning, and Sandy fired her."

Umar paused, then said, "Well, isn't she an alley cat." He hit the printer with his paw.

•

"WINOOONNNAAA!"

Winona jumped. His voice was so loud, so abrupt. She wished he'd rumble or murmur first so she could prepare.

"Yes, Mr. Mauster?"

"I'm falling asleep here. Any chance you could make another pot of coffee?"

"With pleasure," she said. No one caught the funniness of this remark, but Winona chuckled to herself self-indulgently on her way down the hall. Rex was on the phone with his stockbroker making a million dollars on the backs of the workers of America; Nancy was practicing her smirk in a hand mirror.

She returned shortly with a cup of coffee.

"Ah, thank you. Now, Winona, I've got some things for you." Bill reached for his mug, took a long slow sip, expressed his judgment, which was that it was very good, very good indeed (dear). Then he ripped off a few pages from his yellow pad and handed them to her. "We've got three letters there, as well as a memo to Sandwitz to go over by messenger along with the documents listed here."

Winona nodded and attempted a chipper, alert look. She imagined herself as a Pomeranian—maybe a Yorkshire terrier?

Bill leaned back in his chair.

"But in the meantime, we've let go of our friend, Miss Cummings."

"Yes."

"Too bad. Always was a nice girl."

"I thought so," said Winona.

"Though she was given warning, and so standard procedure was followed. Not by you, Miss Bartlett, but by Sandy, I surmise."

He looked down his nose at her.

"Right. Well, I felt that there were extenuating circumstances. And since she's been a good employee for so long—"

"May I ask you something else, Winona? Is it true you

do *not* know exactly what we've sent or received from every client at all times?"

"I keep a copy of everything in the correspondence file, and the chrono file, of course. Sometimes the filing is backed up, or someone hasn't told me—"

"That's no excuse. You should be recording all this on the computer. There are prompts in the new system for this. All you need to do is input, every day, your expectations and accomplishments."

Winona gave him a dead stare.

He continued: "You must understand, this will make things easier for Sandy, but it's really the wave of the future, or so I'm told. Call Jason and find out what to do. It's critical we can count on you, Winona. You have a very important job, do you understand? And as for Lucy, please don't let any bleeding heart tendencies get in the way of business. It's just not an efficient way of doing things, and, in the long run, Winona, it doesn't do anyone any favors." He gave her a look, hovering between doubt, pity, and affection, then harrumphed, put his glasses back on, and got back to business. "Now, I've got one more letter for you. Do you have your pad? No? Here, you can use this. To Ron Blitzen. Dear Ron . . ."

•

Later Winona and Rex were sitting in his office coordinating language on a couple of documents. Winona read hers aloud, while Rex read along on the other silently, stopping Winona when he needed to make a change.

Nancy walked by them and then walked back. She slowed down for a look, but kept moving.

"All eyes around here," Rex said.

"Yeah, almost," Winona said cryptically.

"Yeah," Rex said back.

They went back to the document for a while, legalities asserting themselves in the pale light.

Nancy walked by again.

Winona looked up at her; Nancy's eyes were wide like a baby animal's. Maybe she'd walk straight into a wall. *Bam! Ker-pow!* Her nose would pulse like a red cucumber.

"Want to go out for lunch?" Winona asked Rex suddenly.

Rex threw his pencil in the air, missed it on the downward flight, then said sure.

They walked out past Tammy from CityPros, an oldish white woman with hair the color of mop water. She was wearing a tweed jacket with leather patches on the elbows. She looked uncertain of her role, though Winona had explained it all: Receive. Recept. Receptacle. Reception-giver. The woman had given her a blank, $10.95-an-hour stare.

"Have a nice lunch," she whispered, when they were on their way out. The woman shouldn't have to work at all, Winona thought. She should be allowed to return to the library to read handbooks on equestrian dressage, or write sweet, valiant poetry about men lost at Normandy in a long-ago war.

•

The clown guy was on vacation or at clown school or back in prison: trays were piled up on the edges of tables, and straw wrappers had fallen everywhere like surrendered swords.

Two slices, two Cokes.

"So," Winona said.

"Poor Lucy?" Rex asked.

"Poor Lucy."

"Sandy should pick on someone her own size."

"I let it happen. That was wrong," Winona said.

"Don't kid yourself, Winona. In actuality, I'm sure you had nothing to do with it."

"Yeah, but, I should have known—I *did* know. I should have been able to protect her."

He shrugged. "Lucy's a grown-up. I think she knew what was going down."

Winona stirred her Coke with the straw.

"Listen, Rex. You know what you told me about Sandy and Umar? Up against the wall and all that?"

"Yeah?"

Winona hesitated. She could still smell the lavender from their Day of Beauty; she could see the questioning curls of the cigarette smoke surrounding their bench on the street corner; she could feel the clutch of the diamond watch on her wrist, where the sash was later.

"There were other things, too, that didn't seem right, really, that happened."

"Like what?"

"I probably—I don't know—I thought I was helping her," she began. "A month ago or so she asked me to copy the Lisa Box and Stratosphere files, and I did. She said she was going to talk to Bill and Umar about their strategy. She asked me to copy anything new that came in, too. That's fine and everything, but I don't think she ever spoke to Bill or Umar. I think she just did it for herself. Then once she had me deliver something for her, kind of secretly. And she gave me a diamond watch, too—a watch isn't something she can really use, so it's not like she was giving me something important, but then again, a diamond watch, it's an expensive gift. Anyway, I didn't really question these things because, well, I thought she was nice. Only to discover that she isn't really all that nice."

Rex was looking at Winona in what seemed like an ominous and evil way, as if just over her shoulder was a thick cloud of black, turbulent intention. She felt for a moment like turning around, to see what he saw.

"Jesus, Winona. Anyone can see she's not *nice.*"

Winona's face went hot. "Well, I just thought I'd tell you, since, maybe—maybe she's not exactly on the level."

Rex was staring at his slice like it had grown mold.

"Well? What do you think?"

"I think I should deliver pizza for a living."

"I mean, look what happened to Lucy. She's just trying to make a living, support herself and her child. So I'm wondering: do you think this other stuff means anything—you know, anything bad? Do you think we should tell Bill?"

"Tell Bill?" Rex echoed. "What's there to tell, really? You have no evidence of anything concrete. Do you know the addresses of the deliveries?"

"No, but they were both on the West Side. I think I could recognize it. Yeah, I could."

"Did you look at the documents themselves?"

"No—I wouldn't have done that."

"Of course not," Rex said with a grim smile. "And a watch, big deal. Women are always exchanging things like that. Birthdays, housewarmings, showers—it's all really a girl thing, right?" He picked up his pizza, then he put it down again. "The fact is, Bill's crazy about Sandy, you know that. And the trial is next week. If we went in there now, we'd look like two fools out for revenge."

"Well, Lucy is out of a job."

"Winona, until we know more, I think we better just keep quiet."

"Okay, maybe you're right," Winona said.

"Of course, I'm right," said Rex, winking. "I'm the lawyer."

But she was already being quiet—about her film, anyway, her stalker footage of the beautiful blind girl.

There was a lock of hair falling toward Rex's cheek, an infant curl. It seemed unbelievably far away, as if she could never in a million years reach over and tuck it back behind his ear.

2 ⌐

It was the weekend Liz was going to the cook's version of Club Med or whatever it was, so after work Winona went over to her apartment for the traditional send-off and instruction session.

Liz was throwing things. It seemed to be balled-up socks—either that or small black kittens. Either way, Sniffles was watching the trajectory from her hand to the suitcase with much eagerness. He'd treated Winona with his usual disdain, barking madly as she came in the door, then promptly forgetting her presence.

"How could you think I'm going on this trip to— to— meet a man? I'm going to learn how to cook, dammit! God, I wouldn't pay $695 to meet a man. I could just go down to Scoopies and buy a vodka tonic. That would be more efficient. Men. I'm not looking for men. I want to learn how to sauté vegetables!"

"You don't know how to sauté vegetables?"

"Oh, for God's sake, Winona! You just don't understand. There's sautéing vegetables and then there's *sautéing* vegetables. I am *not* going to meet anyone."

"Okay, sis."

"God. Jesus. All right, Winona, the one new thing here is that Sniffles has really taken to getting ice cubes in his water bowl. I think it's the warmer weather. He just needs a cool, cool drink."

"Uh-huh," Winona said. She was looking out the window to the Chrysler Building, trying to imagine Mauster flying a kite out the window, like Rex had said. "I might bring Sniffles over to my apartment for a night or two, if that's okay."

She said it quietly. It was the kind of thing she might sometimes say just to get under Liz's skin, but today she meant it.

"What? That's crazy! He'd *hate* that. Why would you want to do that?"

"Well, so I could sleep at my own place."

"Oh, my God. What's so *important* about that? A house is just a place to flop. It's nothing. This place is nothing. But to a *dog*. To a *dog*, it's *home*."

Winona sighed and fell down on the bed. "Call me a dog, then."

Liz stopped what she was doing—trying to get the hanging mechanism in her garment bag to unlatch so she could get the hangers in—and sat down next to her sister.

She was still in her work clothes, a blue suit and a white blouse with a Peter Pan collar. Her nails matched her purplish-red lipstick. She placed one hand before her on the bed like the film version of a caring boarding schoolmistress, and said, "Winona, dear. Is everything all right? You're not quite yourself tonight. *Is* everything all right? Really. I'd understand if you were mad at me, and you know, trying not to show it. But why don't you come out and say it? I know I'm going away on vacation and you're not. And I know I did better in school and all that stuff. But that's history. Why take it out on me now? Can't you just—"

"Do what you want?"

"Do what I want?! Do what I want?!"

"Oh, Liz," Winona said. Anyway, all the windows in the Chrysler Building were sealed shut; no one could ever open them.

"What?"

"I'll keep Sniffles here, I promise. We'll play charades."

"God, Winona. You're giving me a heart attack. You know my therapist says I need to relax."

"Yeah."

"You," Liz said, affectionately. "You were always the disobedient one. What was that band you used to listen to? The Runaways? They really *were* runaways, too."

"Liz, I hate to break this to you, but I'm the most obedient person I can think of. I'm a Girl from Connecticut."

"What does that mean, girl from Connecticut?" Liz said suspiciously.

From under the coffee table, Sniffles let out a prolonged whimper.

The air in the city was laced with perfume and motor oil and rotted vegetables. The air in the city, downtown, below Astor Place, felt futile most of the time, but also brooded, alive, like something lurked that you couldn't quite see. Winona held the neighborhood together. This was her butcher, her bakery, the drug treatment center she skirted. This was the black magic/heavy metal shop that she didn't frequent, here was the place she bought pierogies and kielbasa and cucumber salad; here was the place she got oatmeal cookies three for a dollar and ate them with countless cups of tea as she hunched over *The Anxiety of Everyday Objects,* the paper version. These were her neighbors: a man in need of a cigarette; a woman sitting on a step with her ungainly cocker spaniel, both looking like they'd given up girdles for good and were happier for it. Here was the strange office she passed every morning and every night on her way to and from the subway. The gold plaque read: ARCHIVE OF DISASTER: BY APPOINTMENT.

Winona opened the front door to her building Tenement Sweet Tenement. She checked her mail. Nothing no offer from Disney, no fan letter from Al Pacino. She went up the stairs. The stairwell was painted tan, with pale yellow tile steps and an iron banister. Overlaid on the paint were rows of faux wallpaper created with a stencil roller. Whoever did the job didn't really care much about the work; the rows of diamonds, stripes, and paisley wobbled all the way up the wall. A couple of dim fluorescent bars overhead gave the place a throbbing, mothlike pallor.

It had seemed fun when Wendy lived there, too, like they were two extras from *The Rocky Horror Picture Show* and they could get dressed up and sing a cappella and not worry about cockroaches or the future. It was still a pretty good place to write, except for when the aging drug dealer downstairs beat his girlfriend late in the night, or weekend mornings when the exterminator came around, lugging his tin can of chemicals, knocking on everyone's door, "'Sterminator," he'd say, sounding like some kind of David Lynch character, and wait to see if you'd let him in or not. She'd only done it once. She was horrified by the white trail of poison he haphazardly trickled around the edges of her apartment. She tried to clean it up with wet paper towels when he was gone, and for the rest of the week watched Fruit Bat compulsively for signs of distress.

Winona opened up the door and locked it again, took off her jacket. The cat jumped down from his chair and stretched, like he was in no hurry to get to her.

First she washed her hands and face. She lit the votives on her table and put on a CD and took off all her clothes and lay down on the bed, faceup. Her body sunk into the burgundy silk quilt; the flames, behind glass, gained confidence and then remained still. Like most New York City apartments, hers was suffocatingly hot most days, so she always left the window open a crack. The night's trespassing breezes stole across her legs and stomach.

La Traviata.

After a while, she turned on her side, gathering the quilt around her and closing her eyes and wishing for something—she didn't know what. Or she did know what, but she couldn't quite allow herself to go there.

Sometimes sleep really does help. Sometimes the morning—even a Manhattan morning, the air tumbling with incinerator ash, with argument—brings new conviction. When she woke up on Friday, Winona knew that she had to tell Rex about the videotape. If she didn't tell him about it, she was a liar. She could be a lot of things, she could even be an artist/stalker, but she didn't want to be a liar. With Rex in particular.

She got to the office and made the coffee, as usual, but standing in front of the coffeemaker, she felt impatient and panicky. Without even measuring, she dumped a wanton heap of coffee in the filter. She went to Rex's office and asked if she could come in. Of course, he said. She closed the door behind her.

"Be careful now, Big Brother is watching. Or, in our case, Big Sister."

"Yeah. Listen, Rex." Winona walked up to the window, looked out, walked back to the other side of his desk, crossed her arms. "There's one thing I didn't tell you."

"Don't tell me, you're engaged."

His hair was still a little wet at the ends. He was wearing a new blue shirt, with creases across his shoulders.

"I did this thing—whatever. Probably not the greatest thing in the world."

"Yeah?"

"So, you know how I got a new camera and everything? Well, I took some footage of Sandy."

"What?"

"I filmed Sandy. She didn't know it. I did it secretly. Kind of like, I don't know—"

"Like a stalker?"

"Uh, yeah."

Rex didn't say anything. Now Winona stood still and watched him. He was looking at the edge of his desk, or maybe at her coffee cup.

"Wow," he said, finally.

Embarrassment is a peculiar feeling. Was the video of Sandy art, really, or was it just evidence of obsession, a kind of street-theater therapy session? She stumbled back into the conversation.

"Well, I thought it was kind of interesting. The ultimate cinematic eye."

"That sounds way too complicated for me," he said.

"Right. Anyway, I just wanted to tell you. Since we'd been talking about her and everything."

Rex wouldn't look her in the eye. He said: "What was she doing when you filmed her?"

"She was getting a taxi once, working at her desk once, eating lunch with some woman. A friend, I think."

"Well, thanks for telling me, I guess."

"Okay," Winona said. "So, here."

She passed him the tape.

"What?"

"Would you take a look at it? I don't know, maybe there's something in there. Maybe we can make use of it somehow."

"I don't know about that, Winona," he said slowly. He took the tape anyway.

When she left, he put it in a drawer.

•

Well, *that* didn't go particularly well, Winona thought, on the uptown train to Harlem. Still, there was another thing she'd felt she had to do today, and she was carrying through.

After they crossed Ninety-sixth Street, she was one of a handful, then one of two, in the car. She sat with her hands folded on her lap and her gaze focused, not on the old lady across the way who was scowling at her, but at the window—at her own white reflection in the racing tunnelscape, a rush of close walls and reeling wires and rusty wet designs behind the glass. If you could capture just one five-by-five-foot section of this underground and frame it, you'd have a fascinating piece of modern art, beautiful and ugly and filled with what the critics would scrupulously call *frisson*.

When she got off the train, Winona looked in both directions down the platform. She walked toward the EXIT sign, went through the turnstile. This station had been passed over, it seemed, during any recent urban renovations. Hand-stenciled signs reading NORTHBOUND and SOUTHBOUND were screwed into wooden doorframes. Out on the street, she smiled gamely at a man in a crocheted cap and a batik tunic selling incense and scarves and batteries. He might have smiled back, but she wasn't sure. She passed a music store and a soul food store and a wig shop with brightly colored hairpieces, long braids, black hair ironed into amazing pyramids and Mississippi river swirls. A little gang of girls in their early teens came storming up the center of the sidewalk, giggling and gawkily falling into each other, showy and confident. They weren't moving out of the way for anyone, not these girls. They were young superheroes, ready to take on the world.

Here's another New York entirely, Winona thought, less than six miles away from my leftist-artsy/Guatemalan-coffee/blue-martini East Village sanctuary, even closer to the land of frenzied lawyer ballet. Why hadn't she been here before? Why hadn't she even *thought* about coming here? As a filmmaker, she should know this about herself. You had to know yourself to know the world.

She found Lucy's street. An abandoned building—gorgeous once, now boarded up and scrawled over—stood sentinel at the corner. About halfway down the block, she came to an apartment building with a nearly featureless front yard, except for some scrappy, buzz-cut bushes and a Big Wheel lying on the dried grass, knocked over.

Winona opened the gate and walked up the concrete path. A woman much younger than herself came out the door holding a baby in a carrier. She gave Winona a strange look and held the door open.

"Thank you," Winona said, a not-so-New York finish to her words. Holding open the door, she looked for Lucy's name. The names by the buzzers were all marked differently, like an archeological artifact of the city's decline. The oldest names (she assumed) were engraved in black plastic; the recent arrivals were scrawled with ballpoint pen on scraps of paper.

There it was—Cummings. Winona rang the bell. A scratchy version of Lucy's voice emitted from the speaker.

"Hi, Lucy? It's Winona."

There was a pause, then Lucy said, "Winona, what are you doing here?"

She invited Winona up.

On the fifth floor, Lucy appeared in a doorway, dressed in a sweatshirt and jeans.

"Sorry about the broken elevator," she said.

"That's okay," Winona said, out of breath. "This is good for me. Exercise is the opiate of the masses."

Winona opened her bag and started to pull out the catalogs and books she'd retrieved from Lucy's bottom drawer.

"I just wanted to bring you your things."

"You didn't have to do that, Winona."

"No big deal. I told them I had a doctor's appointment. Anyway, I needed to get out of there."

She handed Lucy what she had brought. The ensuing silence was filled by the sound of the television, the traffic, the heater.

"Lucy, I really didn't like the way things happened yesterday."

"Hey, you're not the one who got fired."

"I know but I—"

"You want to meet Denzel? He's home sick today."

"Sure, I'd like that."

The apartment smelled like cinnamon toast and the hall was lined with family pictures. A little boy regarded Winona intently from behind the door to the living room. He was wearing Roy Rogers sleepwear.

"Come on out, buddy. Say hi to Winona. This is a lady I work with—worked with—at the law firm."

The boy shuffled away from the wall reluctantly, walking up to the visitor. He put his hand out formally, ambassador from the land of stuffed animals and toy cars.

"Nice to meet you," he said.

"Nice to meet you, too, Denzel," Winona said, holding the small, warm hand in hers.

Then he turned away quickly and ran full tilt back toward the living room.

"*Aladdin* is on!" he shouted, released and happy.

"One hit of children's Tylenol and he thinks he's Superman."

"He's adorable."

"Isn't he, though? You should see him when he's well."

Lucy's arms were folded around the catalogs.

"Yeah. Well, listen, Lucy, I am really sorry about what happened."

She shrugged. "I know you are, Winona."

"I just wish there was something I could have done."

Lucy didn't say anything.

"I mean, it's just not fair."

"Y'know, Winona, you don't belong at Grecko Mauster Crill. See what I mean? Stay at a place like that and you become part of the problem."

"I know, but—I've got to pay the rent."

"The rent gets paid, Winona."

"Mom! The genie's on!" Denzel called from the other room.

Lucy continued, "I'm not sorry to be out of there. I should have quit that place long ago. And you know what?

I've already got two interviews lined up for next week. Magic, see?"

"Yeah . . ." Winona said.

"Mom!" Denzel called again.

"You have to watch out, that's the thing. A job is just a job—you can't let it steal your soul. You should remember that," Lucy said, then she called back to Denzel: "Cool your jets, bud! I'll be there in a minute."

"Yeah, well, I guess I better go. But Lucy, let's keep in touch, okay? I'm still going to make that lasagna recipe you gave me."

"People don't stay in touch, Winona. That's the thing. But thanks anyway."

Winona tried to protest, but Lucy, still holding the catalogs, gave her a one-armed hug instead. Over Lucy's shoulder, Winona saw Denzel bouncing on the couch, higher and higher. Then she walked the five flights back down to the street.

•

Back at the office, chaos reigned. With the Lisa Box trial coming up next week, everyone was working furiously and at odds and at the last minute and in tandem with each other. Nancy, who seemingly was taking her bill-collector status more seriously than Winona ever had, was insistently talking to someone on the phone about partial payments. Winona could hear Tammy breaking the photocopier in the storage room (anything mechanical frightened her nearly witless, but she didn't let this stop her from trying out the whimsical new technologies), and Bill and Umar were barking at each other about

Lisa Box and Lisa's Lil' Sister and Doug Sandwitz and Ron's last call from either end of the hallway. As for Rex, he was rushing about on winged wingtips. He had sweat on his forehead. She saw it as he flew past her. Only Sandy seemed calm, in a preternatural ice princess way.

Winona grabbed the pile of letters to be typed from her chair and sat down. She wondered if Rex had watched the video yet. She expected not—only Bill had a TV and VCR in his office. Still, Rex was a resourceful guy. Maybe he'd gone to his apartment and watched it. She more than half expected he'd talk to her before the end of the day. Maybe he'd meet her in the lobby.

But at five-thirty, when she was sorting through Tammy's papers for the temp agency, Rex left the office—with Sandy. On the way out, she was telling him something funny, very very funny—about what, Winona couldn't tell. She watched him laugh on the other side of the glass doors to the law office, waiting for the elevator. She and Anthony Grecko watched him laugh.

Winona couldn't fucking believe it. Neither she nor Grecko found anything appropriate about laughter under these circumstances.

•

"Hey, Sniffles."

The front hall to Liz's apartment was quiet, churchlike in atmosphere. Winona switched on the light. The dog looked up at her, frankly disappointed but also practical. He began his dance to get outdoors.

The fur under his chin was softer than the rest. When she latched on the leash, she massaged his hot neck for a minute, cupped his ear in her fingers.

At first she didn't mean to bring him home; she just started walking that way.

"Fruit Bat, Sniffles. Sniffles, Fruit Bat," she said when she got to her apartment.

The cat was glued to the wall at the very edge of the bed. The dog cocked his head at the penury of this part of town.

They'd met before, and in general Fruit Bat found dogs all right, for lesser beings, but still. Winona began to think that Fruit Bat may have preferred to be alone, after all, and the cloud of this thinking mixed with various other clouds until the only choice left for her was to stop thinking entirely. Her ears were actually ringing. She made broccoli and pasta with ferocious concentration.

3 ～

On Monday morning, two days before the trial, the computer had eaten a document, so it seemed, so Winona had to re-create it from scratch. She pulled up a template, changed the font, justified the margins, created headers, then started in on the text. Thirty minutes never went so quickly, never seemed so chock full as they did when her mind was focused on some such vaguely pedestrian act—like she was a horse with blinders. And computers never ate documents more often than when things needed to be done in a hurry.

Then the printer started jamming in a new and mysterious way. She even had to get out the manual. E4? Then G6? And then no error at all, just a little printer icon frozen on the computer screen and an unlistening printer greenly, brightly saying READY but not doing anything. Rex looked in on her on his way to the water fountain. She hadn't spoken to him since Friday.

"Morning, Hepburn," he said.

She didn't say anything.

"Lost the capacity to function, my friend?"

He half crouched by the fountain now, tipping the blue lever, waiting for his cup to fill.

Winona looked at him. Him: Lover of Blind Women.

"Well?" he said.

"The printer won't work," Winona answered, staring forward.

Rex asked about this and that possible problem and remedy—no, no, tried that, no—then he said, "You better turn it off, then. Turn it all off and try again. Some invisible evil has gotten into the system."

"It's not in the manual."

"Some of life's best tricks aren't in the manual. You should know that."

She gave him a look. He didn't seem to understand.

"Well, just turn it off and on again," he repeated. "It's your best shot. Either that or it's a trip down to Forty-second Street Photo for a new one."

He turned and started down the hall. What about their investigation of Sandy, was that entirely over, was Winona on the outside now? And what about her video, the mise-en-scène, the excellent hand-held tracking technique, the through-the-window framing?

"Seen any good movies lately?" she asked. She'd have been more specific, but there were ears, bionic blind ears, everywhere.

"Well, no, actually," he said. He had a stricken look she didn't understand.

She began to earnestly hate him. She thought she'd have a nervous breakdown.

In the conference room, Sandy was luring fragile things into the jaws of destruction.

•

At her lunch hour, Winona made an attempt at writing. Writing was a wonderful hobby, both lulling and invigorating.

The lobby fountains hissed like cats. Uncreatively, and instead of coming up with any lovely images that might evoke certain feelings in others, certain images that welled up inside her like personal truth, like visions, Winona began to wonder about the audience for her film, once it was completed. An audience, after all, seemed important: the underlying idea of communication. Wasn't that really the point? But for her audience, all she could come up with was Liz, Rex, and her parents. Scratch that. Liz and her parents. Fruit Bat and Sniffles in the front, on cushions. A semicircle of four folding chairs and a large bowl of microwave popcorn. Not exactly Sundance.

This is when she saw the orphan, or the ingénue. First, she heard a little *beep* next to her on the bench and looked over.

A girl was sitting there; she had just turned on her cell phone.

The girl had wispy blond hair that had spread, a spider of static, all over her knapsack. She wore a puffy black jacket and absurdly long black pants. Her hand, holding the phone, was small, childlike, and it was that, and her voice, that gave her away.

"Yes? I am inquiring about the possibility of rooms available for sleeping? How much are they? Nineteen? And the bathrooms? Are they in the rooms? Yes, and excuse me? Can you please tell me which subway goes up to East 180th Street? Oh, okay. And which park would that be?"

Winona looked up into the drizzle of the nearby fountain and began to become alarmed. She looked over at the girl again, who was now putting her phone back in her Hello Kitty! purse. The girl took out a cigarette, a Winston, and lit it with a purple plastic lighter. She exhaled a long stream of smoke.

She caught Winona looking and asked, "Do you want me to put this out?" holding the cigarette like the last piece in a jigsaw puzzle.

"Oh, no, that's fine," said Winona. "I like smoking."

"Oh."

They sat there for another minute. The girl probably thought she was some kind of middle-aged ninny. The girl was at the beautiful, fresh beginning of life—and here she was in the lobby of the grand Hyatt . . . doing what? Preparing to go to some hotel in the Bronx? Alone?

"You know," Winona said. "I'm sorry, but I couldn't help but overhear you. Are you by any chance on your own? Do you need anything, like any help or anything?"

The girl started looking around the lobby. She reached toward the sand bucket and abandoned her cigarette there.

"Hey, really, don't worry. I was just wondering. You know, I'm from here. I could help you, maybe, or something. I don't know what."

The teenager got up and said, "I'm outta here."

"Hey, wait a minute, I'm just, I just thought—"

But she had turned away and was hurrying toward the doors to the street. Winona stood to follow her, and the peanut butter and jelly baggie under her leg, now empty, fell to the floor.

•

The next day Winona got up with the alarm, bleary eyed, and shuffled over to the stove to put on water for coffee. She opened the refrigerator and took out a half-full can of cat food. Where was Fruit Bat, anyway? He wasn't rubbing his head against the corner of the wall, against her leg, as he usually did in the morning, making it almost impossible not to trip over him as she prepared his breakfast. She put the bowl down and called him. Still nothing.

He was under the desk, methodically licking between his legs.

"Fruit Bat," she said, pulling the chair away from the desk. "What are you doing?"

The cat stopped and looked at her. Then he got up and began walking toward his bowl. He was holding his tail in a funny way, his back arched and stiff. He went to his dish, sniffed, and turned away again. He walked to the middle of the room, sat down, and stared at Winona, as if she should understand him.

Obviously he was not well. She would call the vet when she got to work and make an appointment. Her damn vet was a nasty bastard, and he charged an arm and a leg for everything. He seemed to have gotten the animal part down all right, but customer interaction was too much for him. Still, she trusted his work, and he took credit cards—and that was all she could pay with at the moment. Winona took a shower and got dressed. She sat on the floor with the cat for a few minutes while drinking her coffee, stroking his head.

On the subway she was jostled, as usual, by all the black-leather jackets getting on at Astor Place. She held the railing. Once, when she had lived near Boston, Fruit Bat had been hit by a car. Not terrible, but when she came home from work that day he was lying on the step, and she knew something was wrong from the way he was holding his body. He'd only broken a rib and torn a muscle in his back leg. She'd had to keep him confined for two weeks in the bathroom. She'd put a princess-and-the-pea amount of folded towels and blankets on the floor for him and had gotten used to sitting in there herself, back against the door, reading.

She got to the office and went right to her desk. She removed the reams of yellow paper drafts and madly marked-up documents from her chair and called the vet, making an appointment for six o'clock. After she hung up, Winona looked behind her: Nancy was there. She held a stack of filing in her hand.

"Cat sick?" Nancy asked.

"Yeah," said Winona.

"I used to show cats, back in the eighties. Maine Coons. I tell you, I had cat fur for breakfast, lunch, and dinner. My husband went a little crazy. That's why I switched to orchids."

Winona smiled tentatively. She and Nancy hadn't exactly spoken lately.

"What's wrong with your kitty?" Nancy asked.

Winona explained the symptoms.

"Winona, that sounds like a urinary blockage," said Nancy, looking genuinely concerned. "That's critical. You can't wait until tonight. I don't want to scare you or anything, but he could be dead within hours."

"What?"

"These blockages can be very serious with male cats. It's not to say that's what he has, necessarily, but—"

Nancy started to explain something about crystals, but all Winona could hear was *dead within hours*. She stared at Nancy, coordinated to the point of despair in light blue; she looked like a 1950s *Good Housekeeping* living room. "If I were you, I'd go now," Nancy was saying.

"Now?" Winona said, looking at her watch, not that she didn't know what time it was. She hadn't even made Bill's coffee yet. "But the lady I talked to at the vet's didn't say anything like this."

Nancy got back her regular tone: "Oh, support staff! Winona, you know how people are! That woman was probably painting her nails and reading a magazine when she was talking to you."

Nancy gave Winona an apologetic smile. Then she hurried back to her office.

Winona sat in her chair, trying to pretend that she was about to start work. She wouldn't have been able to do it, even if she wanted to.

"Good morning, Bill, Sandy," she said, standing in the door.

Bill was reading Sandy a letter and looked up when Winona spoke. "Just set the coffee over here, thank you."

"I don't have the coffee."

"Well, get some, my dear."

"Mr. Mauster, I can't. I have to go now."

"Excuse me?"

"My cat is sick and I need to take him to the vet. I need to go right now."

"Your *cat* is sick?" Sandy said incredulously.

"Winona, don't you think you could take him later, at your lunch hour, or after work? I need you now. These letters need to go out. Honey."

"Yes, you do realize that it's a very, very busy day?" Sandy asked.

"Yes, but—"

"Winona, I need my coffee, and this needs to be typed up and sent by messenger over to Ruck & Staw."

Bill held out a sheaf of papers. Winona didn't move.

"A doctor's appointment in the middle of the day, and now this. Bill? Remember what we've spoken about? Professionalism?" Sandy said. She'd turned her head—was it for show, or was it an old instinct?—in his direction.

"Yes, yes."

Winona looked from Bill to Sandy and back again. She considered going along with the scheme. She would say, all right, she'd get the work done, and it was true, Fruit Bat probably would be okay until lunchtime. *Dead within hours.*

"Mr. Mauster. I am going to the vet—now," she said, a little louder.

Bill suddenly laughed, a guffaw like a cough. "Well,

would you look at this. Okay, Miss Bartlett, why don't you go on, take your cat to the vet. Sure, we understand. But you should realize that if you go, you will not be coming back."

"Fine," she said. She felt like she was on stage. In a film. Being watched.

Sandy cocked her head. The lenses in her sunglasses briefly lit up, a reflection from the window, then went black again.

Winona turned and walked out of the office.

•

The hardest part about transporting the cat in his carrier was that Fruit Bat kept shifting his weight. Every second step the cage thumped into her leg; every once in a while she and the whole ship listed left or right or backward.

"Bartlett. Fruit Bat," she said, when she got there. She squinted at the receptionist.

4 ～

*L*iz trailed her fork over her spinach salad like a divining rod. "It's just too much dressing," she finally decreed, and slid her plate to one side.

They were at a restaurant Winona had never been to before, one of the fancy ones that was beginning to take over the neighborhood. The East Village itself didn't even have a name, once—it was just a place where people lived and went about life. Now it was sporting restaurants with names only the initiated could pronounce.

Winona took another bite of her hamburger. She had a draft ale and some French fries that were called, at this establishment, *shavings*.

The vet had concurred with Nancy: it was a dangerous situation. He seemed outraged, generally, but still, he was on her side. He said they'd need to put a catheter in the cat and monitor him for the rest of the day, probably overnight.

When Winona got back to her apartment—it seemed strangely gray and quiet at that hour, without Fruit Bat— she found a message from Liz. It seemed Tammy had said something about Winona just "up and leaving" and Tammy "had not a clue in the world what was happening in this place." Winona called her sister back and told her what had happened. Liz listened. Liz was good about it. She called back in a couple of hours, as well. Fruit Bat was doing slightly better by then, but they were going to keep him overnight. Liz asked Winona if she could come down to her neighborhood—something she never, ever did— and take her out to dinner. Now here they were, too much dressing on the salad, but still everything was all right.

"So, tell me more about your trip," Winona said.

"I didn't meet anyone. Oh, well."

"I thought you didn't want to meet anyone, that you were going to learn how to cook."

"Of course. I went there to learn how to cook—how could I forget?" Liz smiled at the wall.

Winona went back to her French fries. "You know what, Liz?" she said.

"What?"

"I think you're amazing."

"Amazing?"

"You never give up. You keep trying all kinds of things. No one would ever say you don't have a pulse."

"I'd hope not!"

"Can't say that for everyone," Winona said. "I just think it's cool. In a sister." She watched Liz put on her lipstick. "Thanks for coming down to rescue me tonight."

"No problem, Winona. You'd do the same for me, right?" She said it casually, but there was something in her face that told Winona she wanted to hear the answer.

"Eh," said Winona.

Liz rolled her eyes, but Winona knew Liz knew what she meant.

•

Three blocks west and seventy blocks north, in an apartment sparingly furnished with baseball, film, and comic book memorabilia, with one espresso maker that he'd never learned to use and one tabletop ironing board that he never put away, Rex put the video—finally—in his VCR. He was, let's face it, old-fashioned in some ways, and the whole notion of filming the blind freaked him out. Besides, what could he possibly learn from watching Sandy catch a cab, or eat Caesar salad with some friend?

He clicked on his TV, and there she was, Sandy Spires, making her debut in his living room. Rex grimaced with fascination. Dutifully, he tried to make out what was on her computer. Then that image was replaced, and all the whirl and incandescence of the city filled the television screen. Again there was Sandy, this time slipping into a cab. Fade out. Next, another street scene, this time with better light, less contrast. Sandy was walking away from the camera, a lone wavering figure in the center of the wild city. Faces appeared on the edges of the screen, looked in at him—desperate, hostile—then disappeared.

It was like snorkeling through New York. He was swimming by everything, watching, exhilarated, like Winona had watched.

Sandy stopped in front of a building, a restaurant, and then the image turned dark.

Fade back in, to Sandy sitting at a table with another woman.

Rex breathed in, breathed out, steadying himself.

He knew the woman behind the camera. He was in her head now, looking where she looked: at an intimate portrait, drawn from inside. And, like Winona, he watched the scene unfold once, then again.

The only difference was that he knew both women on the screen.

5 ⌒

*B*ill called her the next morning. "Winona Bartlett?" he said, and at first she didn't know who it was, and thought she had either won a contest or had lost something very important. Then he said it was Bill, and that he was—and he said this gruffly, like he needed to rush through it— sorry about yesterday. He even asked about her cat, um, Fruit Loop? He paused before saying that there'd been some new developments, and they really wanted her back. That he and Umar really wanted her back and would make it worth her while and he'd explain the whole thing to her more fully when she got to the office. Would she come to the office? Could she make it before lunch?

When Winona got off the phone, she hardly knew what to think. She felt reluctant, very reluctant, to put on her pantyhose, but then again she was also surprised—flattered, really—that Bill had called her. To hear Bill Mauster apologize, that was something. They needed her, she thought (imagined?). Today was the Lisa Box trial. The responsible thing was to go back.

Mostly, though, she wanted to see Rex. She wanted to ask him again about the video. But beyond their sleuthing about Sandy, their shared dissatisfaction about what was going on at the office, there was something else. Winona hadn't said good-bye, she hadn't told him what was up. And she wanted to. She wanted to—she needed to—keep in touch. If this thing with Fruit Bat had any redeeming value, it was that it gave her a sense of what was important, and what was not.

•

Tammy, the temp, was wobbling at the front desk, as if her screws hadn't quite gone in all the way that morning. She said, "Greetings," which was what they said in the nineteenth century when secretaries came back into town.

Rex wasn't in his office. That wasn't too strange, not at the moment: he was probably already in court with Umar. But then she saw, down the hall, that Umar was in Bill's office.

She walked down the hall and turned into her own little area—what used to be her area. Bill had seen her, knew that she was here now. He and Umar would be waiting for her.

She stood for what seemed like a long time, but was probably actually just ten seconds, being waited for. Then she joined the men in Bill's office.

"Hello," she said.

"Hello, Winona," Umar said in a gentle way. Bill was giving her a strange, sad look, like her father had given her when she was a kid, before telling her that her goldfish had gone belly up.

"Are Rex and Sandy already in court?" she asked.

"Rex and Sandy?" Umar echoed. "Rex and Sandy, that's a thought."

"It doesn't appear to be the case," Bill said dryly.

"We're not going to trial today, Winona. We settled."

"You settled? But—what about our case?" She looked first at Umar, then Bill.

Bill said: "We were forced to settle, Winona."

"Not a total loss, but still," said Umar. "No Riviera vacations for us. In fact, no extra tubs of blue cheese dressing, not at fifty cents a pop."

"What happened?"

"What happened? That's an interesting question," said Umar. "Well, you could say the morning was full of surprises. Some good, some not so good. Some more colorful than others. The first thing that happened was that Rex stormed in here with a videotape in his hand—your videotape, it seems. It's got some interesting footage on it, certainly. Sandy eating lunch with Brenda, for instance."

"Brenda—Blitzen?"

"Brenda Blitzen," Bill confirmed.

"Fancy that," Umar said. "The Blind and the Beautiful."

"Naturally we had some concerns about this particular pairing," said Bill. "Not to mention Rex's other revelations. Apparently you photocopied some documents for Ms. Spires? This is something you did without our knowledge?"

"I did copy some things for her," Winona said, taking a long, close look at her palms, then looking up again. "She said she was going to help you with your defense."

"Yes, we, too, had certain unrealized hopes. Unrealized expectations," Bill murmured.

"Brutalized. Like little lambs in the forest," said Umar.

"You never met Ron's ex-wife, did you, Winona?" asked Bill.

"No, I never did." She had always thought it would be interesting to meet her, to assess the Stepford quotient. But she'd only heard of Ron's ex, seen her stationery as it scrolled through the fax. Now she tried to put this together with the woman in the tan shawl.

"Any thoughts on where Brenda went to college?" asked Bill.

"She went to college? I guess I thought—"

"No one thought she went to college," Umar interjected. "But she did. At Northwestern. That's where she met Sandy Spires. Well, Brenda didn't last too long at school. After she met Ron, she kind of fell off the intellectual bandwagon, as it were."

Bill said: "Brenda hired Sandy, it turns out, to ferret out information on Lisa Box. Sandy's association with the firm was espionage from the start. She'd never met Ron herself, but she was willing, apparently, to help an aggrieved ex-wife get everything she could from the poor sap. And it turned out Sandy had no trouble at all getting what she came for."

Both lawyers remained intensely glum and silent for a leaden moment. The sky behind Bill seemed heavy and full, the long pane of glass ready to snap from pressure.

Umar leaned forward. "We always expected the divorce to be messy—that's why we were anxious to get this Stratosphere matter out of the way first. But we didn't recognize the extent of Mrs. Blitzen's selfishness, her mental illness. Everyone knows the solutions Lisa Box offers are basically like duct-taping a wound: it only gets worse underneath. I know that. Anyone who knows women should know that." (Umar said the last with a professional's pride.) "Not that I begrudge Ron his wish for a beautiful bride—who wouldn't polish his car before a cruise down Main Street? Still, there are limits, right? I mean, not everyone endures surgeries before marriage. Usually it's just a manicure."

"I guess you're right about that, Umar," said Winona, not sure where this was going exactly.

"It turns out, however, that *this* college-educated woman was mainly interested in her own little pet project."

Bill scoffed. "A pet project? Destroying Ron?"

"C'mon Bill, give the lady some credit."

"What pet project? What are you talking about?" Winona said.

Bill said: "He's talking about Lisa's Lil' Sister, Winona. The charity—well, it was originally Brenda's idea. And now Brenda and Sandy have made some allegations. Brenda claims—hysterically, may I say—that Ron and Leo funneled millions of dollars from Lisa's Lil' Sister into their own accounts. That they used the charity, essentially, to launder profits."

"Hardly any little cleft palates fixed at all. Just a few for show. And a birthmark or two," Umar added.

"I see." Winona made a fruitless attempt to prioritize the ways in which she felt uncomfortable.

Umar let out a huge heaving sigh and looked out the window. "If you're good at what you do . . ." he began, but then didn't say anything more.

Bill said: "We settled with Stratosphere this morning, my dear, because Ron and Leo need to consolidate their power. Brenda's allegations must be kept quiet, or Lisa Box *and* Stratosphere will suffer."

"Straight down. Flames and all. Spectacular, Grecko Mauster Crill-killing fireworks. The sphinx goes down. Paris is burning."

"But did they do that?"

"Do what?"

"Launder profits."

Bill and Umar looked at each other.

"Hey," Umar finally said, giving a big fat shrug. "*Launder?* What does *launder* mean? These are delicate matters, Winona. We don't expect you to understand."

Bill's hands were tightly folded on his desk. "No more than you understood what you were doing for Sandy. No more than you understood what you saw when you filmed her with Brenda."

Winona bristled, but went on. "But what Sandy did is wrong. Illegal. I mean, what makes her think she can get away with it?"

"Sandy is a smart woman," said Bill. "A bitch, maybe. God knows she must have been paid handsomely for this stunt."

Umar crossed his legs, looked at the ceiling. "You want to know what happened, Winona? The woman has it out for Lisa Box. All these women getting their appearances reconfigured. All these anxious women trying to change their beautiful selves. Maybe it pisses her off. They say beauty is in the eye of the beholder, but what if you can't see what the beholder sees? See what I mean? Sandy doesn't understand the rapture of a man. She doesn't know . . ." he trailed off, perhaps momentarily heartbroken, then spoke up again, "how much men can love, really appreciate, the beauty of women."

Bill cut in. "The situation is this, Miss Bartlett. We could take a moment here to express our extreme dissatisfaction with your previous judgment. And we could take another moment to call the district attorney and report our ex-associate, Sandy Spires. But we aren't going to do that."

"But from what I understand—"

"*This* is what we want you to understand," said Bill. "We're going to settle this matter our own way, and Brenda Blitzen is going to keep quiet, and Sandy has gone bye-bye, and we are hoping, very much indeed, that you will make up for what you did to us in a very simple fashion."

He paused, staring Winona down. "Forget any of this ever happened. Forget Sandy Spires—lovely, charming woman that she is. Forget your video. Forget all that. It's over. Stratosphere and Lisa Box have come to an agreement. Lisa Box will continue. Lisa Box will turn over a new leaf."

"If we pursued this, we'd look foolish," said Umar. "And our client would be dealt a mortal blow. And really— well, there's no good in it whatsoever. Once upon a time there was a blind girl, and then she was gone. Ladies across the country keep getting Lisa Boxed. Shrinks stay in business. Life goes on."

"And so if it's not already obvious," Bill said, in his deepest voice, the one he used to lull prey, "we'd like you to come back to work for us. We all need to get back to work. We'll make it worth your while, Winona. And we are, of course, respectfully asking that you, too, keep quiet about all this."

It would have been so easy, at that moment, just to run. After all, she'd already quit once. But on the other hand, she had about forty-five dollars in her bank account, and the vet bill was going to be, oh, ten times that. And weren't they a team? They ate out of the same pretzel box. Her basket of thank-you daisies hadn't died yet.

Besides, quiet was one of her virtues: quiet, happy, kind, diligent. These were the things Connecticut secretaries did best.

"But where is Rex?"

Bill squinted. "The fact is, Rex had to decide on the matter of loyalty. Was his to the firm, to Grecko Mauster Crill, or was it to some abstract notion of—" he paused, as if strong fatigue had taken over—"some abstract, antiquated notion of the law?"

Umar offered his explanation. "Rex is young, Winona. He's idealistic. But who knows where his fury comes from? He may be protesting too much, if you know what I mean. A beautiful woman like Sandy—I may have let something slip myself . . ."

Umar took another headlong look out the window, and then began to scrub his hair.

"The fact remains," said Bill, "they're both gone. But

here *you* are, Miss Bartlett. And we'd like to know we can count on you. You see, you need to think about yourself now."

"But I'm not sure I understand what you're saying about Rex."

"He's gone, Winona. Fade to black," said Umar.

"Trust us, everyone has a dark side," Bill said, looking satisfied.

•

Everyone has a light side, Winona thought to herself, on her way back to her apartment that evening. The cage was heavy and Fruit Bat was bouncing around like crazy, but Winona charged home, filled with some kind of furious, superhuman strength. She couldn't *not* hope, even with the stink of everything, even holding this fucking awkward box, even with the fact that she still had three more blocks to walk and her back was about to give out.

Fruit Bat let out a plaintive sound when she put the cage down to open the building's front door. Through the lobby, the courtyard, up two flights of stairs. When they were back in her apartment and she'd shut and locked the door, she leaned down and opened the cage. He stepped out tentatively, stumbling once, then righting himself. He looked around at his old digs, taking in the concept of home.

They'd pulled out the catheter that morning. He was on antibiotics, and she'd have to feed him some new fancy food from then on. But otherwise, he was all right. He would be all right.

Winona lit her candles. She went into the bathroom and brushed her teeth and washed her face, splashing herself with the warm water again and again, taking in the softness and the soap's fragrance. When she came back out, Fruit Bat had jumped up on the bed and was grooming himself, a fierce post-vet cleaning to rid his fur of all the awfulness there. She went over and scratched him under the ear, and he curled into her hand and flopped all the way over.

She made dinner, pasta and broccoli again, with a few bites of tuna. *Have a seltzer,* she said to herself, as if magnanimous, and poured herself a glass. She read *The New York Times* pretty much cover to cover. When she finished, there were still two hours to go before she could even think about going to bed. She washed the dishes and looked out the window. All day, she'd typed and filed and answered phones; she'd been a patient manager to Tammy, last of her flock; she'd been the person she'd always been for Bill and Umar. Their conversation with her that morning was the lengthiest they'd had since the interview; it was weird to be taken seriously, but they quickly went back to their old ways.

Winona thought about Sandy: about her legs, bent to the side, narrow in black hose, but still shapely, like thin violins next to the rigid line of her white stick. All the time Winona knew her, she'd been someone else. Everything she'd said and done was undone.

Once upon a time there was a blind girl, and then she was gone.

Bill was right about one thing: she had to think about herself now. She still had a job. She needed the money, Winona told herself. She didn't have another job and she needed the money. Later, she'd find another, better job. But for the time being she'd stay. They needed her—or wanted her, anyway. Or wanted her to be quiet. One of those things.

She had felt, at Grecko Mauster Crill, like she belonged somewhere, like when she walked through Grand Central Station in the morning, she and everybody else had something in common. Not like an artist, a crow hunched on a gargoyle taking it all in. She was one of Everyone.

Everyone needs to make a living, she told herself again.

She imagined herself at the office, imagined placing coffee before Bill Mauster, imagined apportioning M & M's to herself: one a page, and an extra five for anything with footnotes. Imagined eating her nine-thousandth peanut butter and jelly sandwich.

When she had—after what had seemed like so long, after what had seemed like years, really—pulled her hands from the sash William had tied, pulled off the blindfold, she had felt, briefly, regret. regret to feel in control again.

You don't really see the sun go down in Manhattan. The ankles and elbows of buildings first acquire these golden hues, these small fires, and then, like sheets of origami, grays replace everything. Blue drains out of the sky and color goes indoors. It's the time of day you don't want to look out the window. The balance shifts from seeing to being seen, and you have no privacy in your speculations anymore.

Everything Winona knew was contained in this one

room. A small collection of condiments. A bathtub. A cat. An address book with the evidence of friends and family, names and numbers. The act of making things real— dialing a number, for instance, listening to another person, inviting that person in—seemed impossible, frightening. She let the address book stay closed. Rex's number wasn't in it, anyway.

6 ⌒

At lunch the next day, Winona walked through the Chrysler Building's lobby, not even noticing, as she usually did, the glamour-dream ceiling, or the frozen-ocean quality of the marble under her feet. Everything seemed plain. Even the glass doors, usually kept scrupulously clean, seemed clouded with fingerprints. She opened one, half-heartedly planning to go to the hotel and stare at nothing.

"Hey there, sunshine."

There stood Rex, in jeans and a pullover shirt, smiling and unshaven by the street corner.

"Rex, what are you doing?"

"Lurking."

"Lurking. I had the feeling . . . I hoped I'd see you again."

"Here I am."

"Here you are."

"Want to get some pizza?"

Indeed. And so they walked back across the street to their favorite pizzeria. The clown was back on task. They sat by the window.

"So," said Winona. "What happened?"

"Didn't they tell you? I quit."

"I quit, too, but I'm still working there."

"I did a better job than you."

"I guess you finally watched my video, huh?"

"Yeah. Hey, you've got talent."

"Thanks. It's one of those little think pieces."

"I wish I'd watched it earlier. I didn't watch it until the night you quit."

"Well, you know, people should look at my work more carefully and more often," Winona said, half-smiling. "Anyway—Brenda Blitzen."

"Brenda Blitzen. Yeah. Wow."

"You should have called me. I had no idea it was her."

"I would have, but—I had this notion. You'd quit under duress, your cat was sick. I figured I'd go in there, get everything taken care of, get you hired back—maybe even get you a raise for your efforts. It was going to be a shining armor moment, Winona. I hadn't counted on Bill and Umar being *genuine* criminals."

"So you quit because of this whole Lisa Box thing?"

"Of course. What, you think I quit because I didn't like the color of my new plaque?"

"You took a moral stand."

"Oh, I wouldn't go that far," Rex said, twirling the pepper shaker. "I'm not *that* bothered by graft, avarice, and betrayal, but—Jesus."

"Rex, is Lisa's Lil' Sister a complete fraud? What do you think?"

Rex stared at the clown. "It's got to be, Winona. If it weren't, Bill wouldn't have folded his hand so fast. We had a *spy* in our firm for two months, after all. If you've got nothing to hide, you'd report a thing like that awfully fast."

He gave her a grim look, slid the pepper shaker back to its spot near the window.

"You think they knew Ron's accounting was wrong, but they were letting it go? That they just let this happen?"

"Seems to be the case."

Winona shook her head. "Well, I guess I'm not that surprised about Ron. But Umar and Bill? That's depressing."

"Yup. It is."

"What did they say when you showed them the video?"

"They were upset, obviously. But I knew something wasn't quite right. After we looked at the tape, I told them about what you'd done—forgive me—about photocopying files for Sandy and everything. All of a sudden they started getting super nervous. Here I was expecting a commendation for saving the day, and within thirty seconds I realized it wasn't going to play out like that at all. I asked what the hell was going on. Bill stared at me like he was going to run me down with a lawn mower, and then—well, we had words, and I was out the door. And soon after that, here I am."

"Here you are."

"She got away with everything."

"Yeah, but it's hard to believe she'd do this for anyone, though—that's the thing. I mean, Brenda and Sandy? I wouldn't have put the two of them together in a million years."

"Well, maybe love is blind," Rex said.

"Love? What do you mean?"

"I actually ran into Sandy yesterday. Purposely, that is. I waited for her in the lobby. I don't know, I just felt like hearing it from her—whatever the hell *it* was. Well, she wasn't entirely forthcoming, as you might have guessed. But when she was talking about Brenda, she seemed— nervous. And sad. And you know Sandy, nervous and sad are not really her thing."

"No, they're not."

"Well, Sandy started talking about the way things had been at Northwestern. She said she was kind of a loner— surprise, surprise—but then she met Brenda. Brenda used to keep her company, I guess. She used to bring her socks and bubble bath—is that, like, a woman thing?"

"Bubble bath is great, but socks? I'm not sure about socks."

"It was the way she was talking about her—I think Brenda really meant something to Sandy. She even said they drank hot chocolate together."

"No way."

"True."

"Sandy, the romantic," Winona said.

"I got the feeling that with Brenda, Sandy let her guard down. The one and only time, is what I'm thinking.

Then Ron Blitzen came into the picture and everything went wrong. Brenda disappeared into the world of Lisa Box and Sandy was heartbroken."

"It's hard to imagine Sandy heartbroken."

"Well, we *do* know that when Brenda called Sandy out of the blue about Lisa's Lil' Sister, Sandy was willing to risk her career for her. And in case you haven't noticed, Sandy isn't what you'd call the altrustic type, as a general rule."

"Yeah, you could say that."

"I think our Sandy was a little peeved that Ron took Brenda away and reconstructed her, literally, into a new person."

"It's so bizarre," Winona said.

But of course it made sense. She could see Sandy touching Brenda's new face, feeling the fault lines there. She could feel the tension of knowledge, the dance of history, as their hands met, then released, when she'd filmed the two women at the restaurant.

Now Winona trailed a finger down her cup. "So the iciest person of all time is susceptible to love."

"Maybe. But maybe she was also testing a theory."

"What theory?"

"She told me she could do anything. People think of a handicap as a sign of weakness, Sandy said, and that's where you get them—like a blow to the knees."

"Jesus."

Rex said: "She knew that if she did it right, there was no way Bill could turn her in—not without destroying his own credibility, and the credibility of the firm. She saw it all perfectly from the beginning."

"Pretty brave."

"Or pretty angry."

Winona looked down at the Formica, brushed away a few pepper flakes. "Okay, this is a little silly I guess, but I have a confession to make."

"You do? What?"

"So you know how you went out with Sandy, that time after work?"

"Yeah?"

"I began to think—I don't know—you and Sandy—"

"No, don't say it. You're crazy if you think—holy moley."

"Okay, so I was a little off."

"Listen, she asked me out for a drink. I figured she was going to work me, like she'd been working you and Umar. Anyway, I thought here's my chance to get some information. I didn't learn much, except that she drinks her martinis extra dry, with one olive."

"Rex, should we report her? Or *them*? What do we have to lose?"

"I'm sure they'd kick our asses if we did. But we could always try it. Or we could just move on."

"We've got the video."

"You mean, we *had* the video."

"What do you mean?"

"Bill wouldn't give it back."

"Really? Hey, shouldn't I get paid for that?"

"If we go after them, we'd never really win. We might prove a point, that's it. What could we win? Money? A medal? And we would definitely lose years of our lives fighting this thing."

Winona studied her cup.

Rex continued: "I myself would just like to go on with my life, I think, and let sleeping criminals lie."

"Right—but I still work there."

"Yeah. Kind of a drag."

"It's not really my dream job, anyway."

"No, it's not," he said, as gently as he could.

Winona smiled and quickly looked out toward the street. After all, she *had* stayed. She'd taken the bait, the offer, to be paid and be quiet. She'd taken the path of least resistance.

A real girl wouldn't do that kind of thing.

"Well, you know what else? You know what's the most important thing, for me?" Rex asked.

"What is it?"

"Now that *I'm* out of there, I can do something I've been wanting to do for a long time."

"Skydiving? Pizza delivery?" she said rather sadly.

"No. The thing is, Winona, I'd really like to see you again. You know? You and me. Will you go out with me again sometime?"

Shafts of sunlight came in, here and there, like ambivalent employees, and it seemed that, lunch hour or not, clown busboy or not, a deep, soft silence had descended upon the room.

"Go out with you?" she said, her voice a near-whisper.

"I know. You said no, before. But I thought I'd at least ask. Ask *again*. You've got to ask again sometimes, to get what you want. You've got to keep asking and asking, you know, because sometimes, sometimes it takes a long time, a long, *long* time—"

"I *would* like to go out with you—again," she said, interrupting him.

Rex looked like he was, for a moment, going to laugh, like he was going down a slide, a dip in the road, and his stomach was in his throat. Then he got serious again.

"Okay, cool, good. Are you eating that?"

"No."

Rex picked up her slice and had a bite. "Pepperoni!" he said, with amazing conviction.

•

Winona went back to the office knowing, even before she got off the elevator, that she would leave. Right then. Without waiting to find a new job. Without waiting for anything.

She finished organizing the Lisa Box/Stratosphere files. She began to subtly finish other things, to put things in order. She threw out her magazines. She deleted the bookmarks from her computer. Around four o'clock, she realized that Mr. Jibbs was up front, shouting at Tammy. She went to the reception area and gazed into his rheumy eyes and wondered again if he had murdered kittens when he was younger, or if he had been a Boy Scout giving out fresh socks to bums in the Bowery. It didn't matter; he still got mystifying letters from the government, and Umar still took time out from *Penthouse* to give him the help he needed.

She walked back to the conference room. The cleaning people had done their job: the stampede of footprints under Sandy's desk was already gone, lost in a pleasant swirl. Winona stepped up to the glass and looked out, now, at New York.

Hundreds of secretaries were looking out windows

like these this very minute, not to mention over the years. The windows were locked against the seduction of despair, but they did allow for dreams.

It had been good in a way, being a secretary. It had given her a parameter. The work was like some ancient rite, like picking grass strands out of a bucket of nails. It required patience and modesty and work for the sake of the thing. It required verve.

Good-bye, secretaries. Good-bye, noble old guard— seamed stockings, kid gloves, Remington-strong fingers, thumbs that could knock a man out—and the pinkies! You could hang laundry from one of these women's pinkies, that's how strong they were. A smudge of mimeograph purple was their tattoo from the Industrial Age. These goddesses were still around—not the originals but their near sisters, available to take a letter without complaint. Mrs. Childs. Mrs. Simms. Mrs. Carryover. Formidable family lives, convictions they kept to themselves, a passion for propriety, and no real sense of humor. They were still out there, typing, answering calls, writing down messages on pink pads in woman-script, anonymous, without flourish, stilted and sexless but easy to read.

And then there was the younger set. Good-bye, brilliant women in bright floral dresses and sophisticated mauve sweaters, women bursting away from their desks, believing they can excel through hard work, sometimes going on cleaning/organizing binges, sometimes swamped in piles of things things things to do, but still confident, even after months, sometimes years, of keeping their desks clean, that they will, if they continue, get somewhere—that they will conquer the world. Good-bye drinks with the girls at TGIFriday's (not that Winona had ever done that, but still). Good-bye blue vases from Crate & Barrel and framed photos and beanbag animals hanging lethargically from computer monitors. Good-bye smart, self-assured, always hopeful peers.

•

"Hey, Nancy," Winona said, on her way out.

The purples, pinks, and yellows on Nancy's windowsill were like the ears on delicate goblins, waiting to hear whispers. Nancy herself was wearing a bright yellow suit that resembled the fur of a bumblebee. All day she'd been in a panic; she'd even asked Winona what she thought of a little Mexican fiesta, something to "heighten staff morale," later in the week.

"Going home? That time already?"

"I am, but before I do, I just wanted to say, again, thank you. I can't tell you how much I appreciate what you did for me. My cat's alive because of you."

Contrary to what you might think, it's hard to look genuinely cheerful in a bumblebee outfit. But Nancy, for a second, really did look glad. Winona thought about saying good-bye, good-bye for real, but she decided against it. She put the CityPros Rolodex card on her keyboard and headed out the door.

7 ～

Winona heard the buzzer ring and told Rex she'd be right down. She met him on her broken-down front step. The brick buildings surrounding the basketball court across the street were fiery with streaks of sunlight. They began walking toward the river.

Somebody's dog was barking ferociously not too far away. A Spanish radio station crackled from an upstairs window. They made their way through a sparkle of broken bottles as they passed Avenue B, then C.

"So, I quit," she said.

"You did, huh? That's great. I'm glad, Winona. Very."

"Yeah. Second time's the charm."

"Yeah," he said. "So, now you'll have more time to make your movie, right?

"Right—until I'm evicted, I guess. I don't know, I'm thinking coffee shop? Either that or encyclopedia sales."

"Yeah, well, hey—I'm thinking mafia, or maybe the government. At least now we can, I don't know, start again. Clean."

"Yes," she said.

They fell silent again. It was easy, because the city took over. They walked across the overpass to the park and there was the East River, glinting sourly, like an alligator on a hungry afternoon. Brooklyn looked great from there. The whole thing looked like something out of those New York City picture books—the ones that don't show any rats.

They stood side by side, studying the horizon.

In her movie, all her shots were small, like boxes, like she was shutting things out as much as seeing them. It was always a cup or a candle or a foot or something. *The Anxiety of Everyday Objects*—could she have a wider angle on these things? Did it have to be the neon sign that says EXIT DANCING instead of EXOTIC DANCING, or could it be something else, something more, well, complete? And this man, Rex. The lawyer. If she made movies, if she really did that, if she really *was* that, Winona the filmmaker, as opposed to Winona the secretary, then it didn't matter anymore if he was a lawyer. What was wrong with law, anyway? (Don't ask her that right now.)

Winona began to feel that she'd had something she'd been fighting, and now it was taken away. She no longer had to resist her identity.

"This," she said finally, sweeping out her arm. "This would make a good movie."

"I think so too, Win," said Rex. He smiled at the sky and the buildings.

•

After a while, they walked back to her neighborhood. They ordered take-out from the nice Italian restaurant on the corner of Fourth and Second, and she'd never done that before and it felt funny and kind of great. The air was warm and fragrant and inside the restaurant was busy. They had opened up the doors to the street and people were eating on the sidewalk.

While they waited for their food, they bought a bottle of Chianti, and then they went back, loaded up, to her place.

Winona opened her door. She turned on the light, walked to her desk, walked back. Here he was. In her apartment.

Rex had put the food down on the counter. He crouched, holding his hand out.

Fruit Bat was sitting in the middle of the room. He looked like a small black and white butler, the one who knows all the family secrets. He regarded Rex, then deigned to get up and walk over to him. He sniffed Rex's hand, thought for a second, gave it a quick sideways rub, and walked away.

"He likes you," said Winona, arms folded tightly.

"Who doesn't?" said Rex. "Well, I guess a couple of lawyers called Bill and Umar, but other than that, I'm quite popular."

"Yeah. I guess they don't think much of me, either."

"Oh, well, who cares? We can always be loved by, like, I don't know, the guys at UNICEF."

"Yeah. Hey, that food smells fantastic."

"Yeah," Rex said. "Hey, this is a nice place."

"Thanks. I like it." Winona sat down on the couch, then got up again. Was it hotter than usual in here?

"So, do you have a corkscrew?"

"Sure—right there, there it is."

He turned toward the kitchen and made sort of a pantomime of discovery.

"We can toast unemployment," Winona said, suddenly.

"Great," said Rex.

It was that time of night when windows become purple. Winona closed the curtains. Then she stood and watched Rex, his bent head, his shoulders: he was working the cork now.

She could have waited, that might have been the polite thing.

She came up behind Rex. She placed her shoulders, her breasts, her stomach, her hips, her thighs, her arms, against the back of him, in shifts of heat, until he turned. Then she looked at him, at those highly unusual, often unsung, green eyes. She trailed her finger over the edge of his ear—like a seashell. She touched the shape of his arm and something new started in and she pressed harder, from her hips and thighs, and their lips met, and they closed their eyes and fell together into a darkness edged with light.

Life was teeming with people, with possibility, and there was some kind of very remote chance, Winona began to think, that this was Happiness, not Anxiety.